THE WORDS THAT FLY BETWEEN US

Also by Sarah Carroll

The Girl in Between

THE
WORDS
THAT FLY
BETWEEN
US

SARAH
CARROLL

SIMON &
SCHUSTER

First published in Great Britain in 2019 by Simon & Schuster UK Ltd
A CBS COMPANY

The Words That Fly Between Us receives financial assistance from the Arts Council.

3 5 7 9 10 8 6 4 2

Simon & Schuster UK Ltd
1st Floor, 222 Gray's Inn Road
London WC1X 8HB

www.simonandschuster.co.uk
www.simonandschuster.com.au
www.simonandschuster.co.in

Simon & Schuster Australia, Sydney
Simon & Schuster India, New Delhi

A CIP catalogue record for this book is available from the British Library.

PB ISBN 978-1-4711-6064-6
eBook ISBN 978-1-4711-6065-3

Typeset in Goudy by M Rules
Printed and bound by CPI Group (UK) Ltd, Croydon, CR0 4YY

Book two, baby two,
Sadhbh, mo chroí,
this one's for you.

Words can be sticky. They nudge their way into the grooves of the tiles, and get wedged in tiny cracks in the plaster, and seep into the grain of the floorboards. And they stay there. If you look closely, you can see them. Our house is filling up with them. People don't realize, though. They think you can just fling them around.

SATURDAY

CHAPTER 1

I hate when Mum and Dad fight. Dad says they don't, they have heated debates. *Your mother gets heated while I debate.*

I'm with my sketch pad and pencil in the nook by the window in the living room. I'm not drawing anything in particular, really.

'Did I tell you, "Don't get white wine"?' Dad says from behind the double doors into the kitchen.

Mum must have made a mistake with the order for his party tonight.

'Yes. You said you only wanted red—'

The higher Mum's voice goes the flatter Dad's stays. 'Did I say, *don't get white.*' He's doing that thing where he rolls the words around in his mouth before he spits each one out, just to be sure that there can be no mistake.

'Here, look ...' She's probably pointing to the piece of paper she's carried around all week. It's been opened and folded so many times it's beginning to tear along the creases. She's right, there was no white wine on the list. 'You wrote down—'

'I'm aware I didn't specify that you should buy white wine. I didn't specify that we needed toilet paper either. Should I check the toilets?'

I know Mum's searching Dad's face right now, looking for just the right words. No more. No less.

'Should I go out now . . . ?'

'Oh, forget it, Alice.'

An intimate get-together, Dad had said. *Starting around seven-thirty. Mr Reynolds will be dropping in.*

Mr Reynolds, who practically owns the bank.

No fuss. Just enough hors d'oeuvres to keep the shareholders from dropping dead with hunger, so to speak. Four trays from Donnybrook Fair should do the trick. And champagne, of course. We'll take one . . . No, wait, better make it two truck loads of the usual. I realize I'm sketching Dad as he'll look in a few hours, big smile, waving a fancy bottle around. *We're a champagne house, ha, ha. What's that, you're not a champagne drinker? Not to worry. Paula here will pop open a delicious little red. Oh, pardon me, it's white wine you're after . . . but . . . but . . . there is no white . . .*

Catastrophe. The whole night ruined. Dad's head explodes. I don't draw that.

'You've had all week, Alice. I've so much on my plate, and I asked you to do one thing . . .'

The kitchen double doors open and I sit on my sketch pad

so Dad doesn't see. Wasting time drawing is bad enough. But I definitely don't want to be caught drawing *him*.

He's already in his suit and a bright pink tie. His *fun* tie. He folds one door back so it's flat against the wall. He sighs and shakes his head.

Mum is standing behind him. She's wearing her red silk dress. She's had her hair curled and has her diamond earrings on too. After a while, she looks up. 'Actually, I think there's a box of leftover white in the cellar.' Dad acts like he hasn't heard her, so she says, 'I'll go check.'

When she's gone, Dad disappears through the kitchen too and I relax back against the wall.

It's got worse since he won that contract for The Old Mill last Christmas. It's like underneath, things started turning bad, but from the outside you can't see. Like an apple getting eaten up by a tiny worm. If you look closely you can see the hole, but that's all.

Take yesterday, for example, when Dad couldn't find his golf shoes. Mum swore she left them on the washing machine, and she ran around looking for them while Dad stood in the kitchen shaking his head and complaining that she was making him late for golf with potential investors.

In the end, Dad found them in the conservatory. He grabbed them and left without saying anything else because he was in too much of a hurry.

When he was gone, Mum went into the conservatory and stared at the spot where he had found them. She said, *I was sure I left them on the washing machine* around seventy times.

Thing is, so was I. Because I saw her leave them there.

I know it was only small, but things like that happen all the time since Dad *moved into the big leagues*. And the longer the development of The Old Mill is delayed, the more stressed Dad gets.

It's usually Mum that he gets annoyed with, but sometimes it's me. And even when everything seems fine, you're just waiting for that moment when the air sours. That's why I hide my sketch pad. So he doesn't give me that look – the same one he gets when he stands in dog dirt. Like I'm a disappointment. Or worse.

The side door to the front hall opens. Our cleaner, Paula, steps into the doorway and holds a champagne glass up to the light. She rubs at a smudge that's not really there. She probably polished the wine bottles too. *A great little cleaner,* Dad calls her. Mum calls her a Duracell battery.

Paula says, with her kids in school, she's ready to do something different. So she's studying at night. But not tonight.

'Have you eaten?' she asks me.

'Yup,' I say.

She looks over the top of the glass at me. 'Washed?'

'Scrubbed,' I say.

'Good woman.'

She leans in a bit so she can see through the double doors. 'What was that about?' she whispers.

'Mum didn't buy white wine,' I say.

Paula lifts an eyebrow. 'He didn't ask for white.'

'I know,' I say.

Now she lifts the other eyebrow. 'And there's loads downstairs.'

'I know,' I say.

Mum comes back into the kitchen, carrying a box, walking like a robot because she's trying not to trip in her high heels. 'Found some!' she calls and she tries to put the box down carefully. But when she looks up, she sees Dad's gone, and her words, and the box, drop with a thump onto the marble countertop. After a second, she claps her hands together and looks down at her dress to make sure it's not smudged. I hop up to help but Paula says, 'Stay where you are, honey. It's covered in dust, you'll ruin your clothes.' She goes into the kitchen where Mum is saying, 'Knew we had some.'

Dad comes in the other door behind them. He pulls a bottle out and turns it over to read the label. He sighs like his best friend, Oly, just died. 'Best we can do, I suppose.'

Paula takes the bottle from his hand and whisks the box out of Dad's way.

Dad comes back into the sitting room. He looks around at the platters and bottles and glasses on the tables. He plumps the cushions on the couch and runs a finger over the mantelpiece. He's checking to see if anything is out of place. But there's nothing wrong. Everything is gleaming.

He notices me sitting in the window nook.

'Ready?' he asks.

I nod.

Then he says, 'At least someone is.'

Who are his words for? They're standing in the air like a glass of wine that someone was supposed to grab. But no one gets to them in time. They drop to the carpet and spread out in an invisible stain. That's why the carpet's so thick: it's filled with words that no one wants.

'You better go get ready.' I look up. He's talking to Mum, even though she's been ready for over an hour. Her mouth drops open a bit. She looks down at her dress, then back at him. He breathes in deep and sucks up all the air in the room. Then he goes over to the couch. Reaches down behind it. Lifts something. It's a box. He hands it to Mum. Her hands are shaking a bit when she takes it. I'm leaning forward, as if that's going to help me see better. All I can think is, *Please let it be nice. Please.*

She lifts something out and the first thing I think is that it's armour, like the chain mail stuff that knights used to wear. It's not. It's a dress. Silver and sparkly, in a really, really expensive way.

'Try it on. It should fit,' Dad says.

'Declan . . .' Mum says. Her shoulders relax a bit.

And the air rushes back into the room again. I breathe it in.

'God, it's just gorgeous,' Mum says.

'It would want to be. Cost nearly three grand,' he says.

'Three grand!' I say. I didn't mean to, the words just came out.

Dad turns. But he laughs, too. He's having fun now.

'Why not?' he says. 'We have the money.' He looks at both

of us like our cat used to when he jumped in the window and plonked a dead bird down in front of us. 'Mr Reynolds is going to be here,' he says.

'Thank you,' Mum says and holds it up against her. She looks so happy that, for some reason, it makes me sad.

'You. Are. Welcome,' he says. Then he holds up his arm and shakes his wrist so his Rolex slides down.

'Go on, go get changed.'

Mum rushes off. Dad surveys the room again and then goes into the hall.

I hope the dress fits. And I hope Dad stays in a good mood.

CHAPTER 2

The guests are all here now. Through the gap in the double doors, I can see them. They're not even all friends with Dad because he had to be introduced to half of them. Imagine having to invite people you don't even know to a party?

'How is it sounding in there?' Paula asks from behind me.

'Loud,' I say.

'Good,' she says. 'As long as they're cheery and full of cheese balls, my job's done.'

'Dad's telling a funny story,' I say.

When I turn, Paula is lifting an eyebrow like she's saying that she seriously doubts it, and I laugh. But it doesn't matter if it's funny. It just matters that Dad thinks it is. Because if he's telling a funny story, it means he's in a good mood.

He's speaking to a group of five men standing in a half-circle beside the food table. He's pretending he's talking to everyone. But he's facing Mr Reynolds.

Now Oly's butting into the story. He always finishes Dad's sentences. He calls himself Uncle Oly, but he's not my uncle. He's like Dad's sidekick in superhero films. Except he's bald and he can't run up walls. I doubt he can even run. He wouldn't be great at chasing super villains. He could probably bore them to death, though.

Beside Oly is Mr Reynolds. Mr Reynolds has loads of hair. It grows out of his nose and ears, and his eyebrows nearly reach his cheeks. I wonder does he walk into things, like those little dogs that can't see because their hair covers their eyes? Him and Oly should do a deal. Oly could take the hair from Mr Reynolds's ears and stick it to his head.

Stepping away from the doors, I jump up on a high stool and grab my sketch pad again. I start to draw Dad's face. He looks different when there are people around. It's like he's in the middle of inventing a really fun game that everyone is going to love.

After a while, next door erupts and I imagine Dad's grin, big enough to take in everyone in the room.

On the countertop, my phone beeps.

Megan
I'm so bored I might even read a book.

Me
The one I read from the summer reading list is
actually good.

Megan

Joking! Not THAT bored.

Me

I am. Dad's parties are like a real life game of
Monopoly. I hate Monopoly.

Megan

That's because you're terrible at it.

I am. But it's a stupid game. Either you're lucky and you get
rich or you're unlucky and you end up broke.

Dad always wins when he plays. Maybe some people are
just good at getting rich.

Megan

Can't believe school starts in three weeks. Ugh! BTW
Hazel is meeting us tomorrow. What time should I
call over?

I don't really know anyone else going to our new school, but
Megan is friends with Hazel from their orchestra and she'll
be going. Hazel actually lives on our road too. We're at one
end, Hazel's house is in the middle, and Mr Reynolds lives
at the other end. Millionaire Square, Dad calls it.

But I hardly ever see Hazel. And the few times I did meet
her, I didn't like her.

Me

Whenever. Just not too early.

The double doors open and Dad comes in with another guy that I've seen at these parties a few times. He's tall and skinny and always nodding.

'Invest now,' Dad's saying, 'and you'll treble your money by the time the foundations are in, guaranteed.' He must be talking about The Old Mill again.

Dad's by the sink grabbing a bottle of champagne from the ice bucket before I remember my sketch pad. I snap it closed, but there's nowhere to hide it. He notices. He watches me for a second, and I imagine the grinning face I drew burning through the front cover. At least it's a picture of Dad in a good mood. But then I remember that a few pages beneath is a drawing of Dad yesterday morning when he couldn't find his golf shoes.

He stares at my pad.

I stare at the countertop.

Then he says, 'So this young lady won a national art competition!' When I look up, he's beaming at Bob. His shoulders are square with pride and he comes over and puts his hand on my head. 'Thousands of other kids entered – and our Lucy won.'

Our Lucy. Our. I inhale the word and it warms my chest.

'With a drawing of the freak who lives next door, no less!' Dad adds.

'Well done, Lucy. That's impressive,' Bob says.

'Yeah, it is,' Dad says.

Dad grins at me, and now I'm smiling too. But his eyes stay on me. I think I'm supposed to speak.

'I actually came second,' I say.

Dad's grin stiffens. I don't think he wanted me to say that.

'The theme was *Hidden*,' I say, hoping that's better. 'So I drew a picture of Ms Cusack next door, or, I mean, what I think she looks like, because she doesn't go out.'

Now Dad's eyes move to Bob. 'That house is practically falling down,' he says. His hand drops from my head and he fills his glass. 'Ruins the whole street. The gap in an otherwise perfect set of teeth. It's a crying shame. I could buy it off her in the morning for two million, and flip it for four by dinner.'

Bob nods around seventeen times. Then he points to my sketch pad. 'Can I see your pictures?' My eyes dart to Dad, but he is putting the bottle back in the wine cooler and doesn't realize what Bob means.

'Not unless you go up to the gallery, I'm afraid,' Dad says. 'They hung her entry up there with Rembrandt and Vameer, I'll have you know.'

'It's *Vermeer*, Dad, and it's not exactly hanging in the same room,' I say, ignoring Bob's arm which is held out towards my pad. Thankfully, by the time Dad turns back, Bob has dropped his arm. Dad takes a drink and looks at the wall like there's something written on it. Then he says, 'There was nothing like that in my day. The emphasis in schools is completely different now. I mean, it's bad enough that Art is treated like an actual subject and not just a hobby, but Lucy will have the option to take Drama this year too! Now a competition that awards initiative? *There's* something I could really get behind. Something . . .'

I turn away from Dad. And I wait for the word. Because I know it's coming.

'. . . *practical*,' he says.

Bob nods. 'Couldn't agree more.'

Dad talks to Bob about the need for children to get real life experiences and I look at the floor tiles and force myself to count the corners and look for cracks and by the time I feel a hand on my shoulder, Dad and Bob are gone. All that's left in the kitchen are me, Paula, and the words Dad didn't say.

Drawing is not a real talent.

'Lucy,' Paula says and she waits for me to look her in the eyes. 'I took my daughter to the gallery to see the portrait you drew. I asked a woman who works there about it. You know what she said? She said this year's entries prove that the next generation are not just very talented, but surprising. That's you, Lucy. Talented and surprising.'

But her words mix with Dad's and form a lump in my throat. I shove my sketch pad away and go out of the kitchen.

CHAPTER 3

I'm not supposed to go down into Dad's precious wine cellar. Which is why I do. I walk along the rows, sliding the bottles out one by one.

'Practical,' I say. The word sits on the heavy air and doesn't move.

Practical. Like making the hockey team or winning the Young Scientist of the Year Competition or running your own property development business. Not winning an art competition.

I reach up and slide out his most expensive bottle.

I don't want to see you down there, young lady. Those bottles of Domaine de la Romanée are worth more than fourteen thousand apiece.

What's practical about a fourteen thousand euro bottle of wine? All I have to do is open my fingers and let it drop and smash! Fourteen thousand euro spills across the ground.

The door to upstairs opens. The music gets louder, there are steps on the stairs. I freeze.

'. . . so, after the jigs and the reels, and the palms that needed greasing, I finally have my hands on two bottles.'

It's Dad. I slide the bottle back and sprint to the end of the wine racks and duck behind them.

'Needless to say, I've paid about twice their original price at this stage.'

Their feet are on the floor of the basement now.

'Hmmm, where are they?' Dad says.

'Up there!' Oly says.

'Yep, that's them!' Dad says and I hear him slide a bottle out. 'Domaine de la Romanée.'

'What's going on with my ten million?' someone says. Who was that?

Through a gap in the racks I see Oly and the arm of another man.

'Your money is coming,' Dad says. 'As soon as The Old Mill— '

The other man moves. It's Mr Reynolds. 'What . . . has The Old Mill . . . got to do . . . with me?' Mr Reynolds asks.

'Nothing. Nothing at all,' Dad says.

'Exactly,' Mr Reynolds says. He smiles. But it's a smile like a scorpion's tail. 'You think I don't know what this little party is really about? You need investors. You're in too deep, Declan. And every day that the development of The Old Mill is delayed, you are sinking further and further.'

'No, not at all,' Dad says. 'Actually, I'm very confident—'

Mr Reynolds holds up his finger and jabs Dad's words with a full stop. 'I don't care about your little problems.' His finger is so close, Dad's going cross-eyed looking at it. 'But if I don't get my money back in one week, Declan, you will find every door to every bank nailed so tightly shut, you won't be able to get so much as a car loan in this city. Do you understand?'

When Dad doesn't reply, Mr Reynolds's voice goes from grey to black. 'Do you understand, Declan?'

'Yes. Seven days,' Dad says.

Mr Reynolds nods. Then he reaches out. His fingers curl around the bottle in Dad's hand. His Domaine de la Romanée. He takes it from him, shakes it in front of Dad's face and says, 'Seven days, Declan.'

He walks away. With Dad's bottle. And Dad doesn't stop him. The slow footsteps reach the top of the stairs. The music gets louder as the door opens. Then it's quiet.

Dad kicks the wine rack and a thousand reds rattle. I have to force myself not to jump, to stay dead still.

'How much am I down?'

'Twenty-one ... nearly twenty-two million,' Oly says. 'That's not counting what you might lose with these new delays.'

Dad owes twenty-two million? Twenty-two *million*?

Dad curses. 'We have *got* to flip this thing.'

Oly looks like he wants to hide under a table. But then Dad points furiously like he's made up his mind about something.

'I'll get five off that idiot Sean, he's itching for a piece of it. I'll find another five off . . . someone. That'll do for paying back Reynolds. Then, we'll get this development moving, flip it, and everyone will get their money back. No one will ever know.'

Oly is nodding the way people always do to Dad. To keep him happy. 'Yep. That's right. Nothing to worry about.'

It's quiet. Dad's pacing. I only catch glimpses of him. Oly is watching him. 'It's just . . .' Oly says and his words trail after Dad.

'What?' Dad says.

'It's just . . . the *legality* of taking Sean's money to pay Reynolds is . . . *questionable*,' Oly says.

Dad spins around. 'Oh, don't pussyfoot around.' Oly ducks and Dad's words hit the wall behind him. 'It's not questionable, Oly. It's *illegal*. And if you have a better solution, by all means, be my guest!'

Oly keeps his head down. Then Dad seems to remember that he needs to wrap his words in cotton wool for people that aren't me or Mum because he says, 'Look, if I temporarily redirect some funds, someone would have to examine the books with a fine tooth comb to figure it out. And unless that someone knows what they're looking for, *specifically* looking for, they are not going to notice.' He comes closer to Oly. 'It'll be fine.' Dad waits until Oly looks up and then offers him a smile as big as a hug. 'And if it does come out, I'll just have to skip the country. Worse places than Brazil to hole up for a while!'

This weird look runs over Oly's face, like he doesn't

believe Dad's saying those words. But like a breeze through grass, it's gone just as quickly. 'Yeah,' Oly says. 'Yeah, okay.'

The music from upstairs suddenly gets loud. Someone opened the cellar door. A voice shouts, 'Declan, Oly? Don't tell me you are getting into that Romanée without me!'

'It's Bob,' Oly whispers to Dad.

'Don't worry, Bob,' Dad shouts. 'You'll be nowhere near this house the day that's popped!' Then Dad and Oly run up the stairs, the cellar door slams and . . .

Silence.

I stand straight.

The air is thick with the echo of their words. They drift through the room before burrowing into the stone wall.

'Questionable,' I whisper. The word slides along the bottle of wine in front of me and when it pops out the other side, it has changed. It's not *Questionable* any more. It's *Illegal*.

CHAPTER 4

I'm sitting on the bottom of the stairs in the front hall waiting for the guests to leave. One by one, they step outside and the hot air from the hallway leaves with them, and all the words that were said tonight, all the jokes and opinions and stories that don't matter any more, slide out of the open door and dissolve into the breeze. Only the heavy ones stay. I imagine them clinging to the carpets and sticking to the lip-stained rims of glasses.

Below us, though, the words that were spoken in the cellar stay where they burrowed and don't budge an inch.

Illegal. Dad said he would take money from Sean to pay off Mr Reynolds and that it would be illegal. Then he smiled like it was no big deal. Like he was talking about ten euro. Not ten million.

'What's more important, Dad?' I whisper too quietly for anyone to hear. 'Practical or legal?'

Mr Reynolds is kissing Mum goodbye.

'You'll be okay walking all the way back on your own?' she says.

'As long as Ms Cusack's not out husband hunting,' he says and Mum laughs.

'You know her?'

'Knew,' he corrects her. 'We are the only two left that grew up on this street.'

'She never married?' Mum asks.

He laughs like it's a silly question. 'No, she's a spinster through and through.' He buttons his jacket closed. 'She's not so bad herself. But the people she surrounded herself with? Wasters. Once the money ran out, so did her friends.'

Mr Reynolds is the last to shuffle out of the front door. Dad waves after him like they are the best of friends and it's really hard to tell that the smile he's wearing is fake. But he slams the door on it and when he turns for the sitting room, his forehead is creasing into frown lines.

I stay on the stairs. Mum goes straight into the living room and collects glasses from behind curtains and under chairs. At the mantelpiece, Dad picks up his whiskey.

'Well, that was a success,' Mum says. When every finger is clutching the rim of a glass, she walks towards the kitchen. That's when he says it.

'*You* certainly seemed to have fun.'

I jump up and go to the living-room door. And I realize why I've been sitting here. I wasn't waiting for the guests to leave. I was waiting for this.

Mum flinches. Just for a fraction of a second. But she knows what's coming too. It's like waiting for a polaroid to develop. The picture has been taken. And the world moves in slow motion as the picture crystallizes.

Mum goes to the sink. 'Yeah, it was nice. Julia is great fun.' She's looking for just the right words to stop the picture from developing. But there are none.

She starts loading the dishwasher.

Dad looks like Mr Reynolds in the cellar earlier. His smile is a scorpion's tail. 'These parties aren't games for your amusement, Alice.' He stands straight again. 'Going on and on to Mr Reynolds about the two years you spent at a financial firm! Honestly, the poor man.'

'He asked me!' Mum says.

'He was being polite! You think the head of one of the largest private investment banks in the country cares about the two years you spent as a junior accounts manager?' Dad grabs his glass and marches towards the kitchen. Mum stumbles backwards when he reaches the sink.

He chucks the rest of his drink into the basin and turns for the dishwasher. He's right in front of her and she's not moving, and he reaches out and grabs her arm hard. 'Alice, get out of my way!'

He doesn't mean the dishwasher. Not really. I take a few steps towards them. I want to yell, 'Let her go,' but I can't. The words are stuck inside.

Mum yanks her arm free but the force of it makes her stumble backwards again and in the next second she trips and falls. She reaches out to stop herself but her head knocks against the countertop.

'Mum!'

But he already has her, his arms lifting her until she's standing upright. 'Are you okay?'

She's holding her head where she bumped it and he's shaking his, like this is all her fault. She steps back and she doesn't look at him. Now he's taking ice from the wine bucket and wrapping it in a tea towel. He's holding it out for her.

For a second no one moves and the tea towel hangs between them.

Say something, Mum.

But she takes it. She holds the ice to her head and he talks like his words are a blanket over a fire. 'You always overdo it at parties . . . I could see it coming all night.'

I want to say, *She was fine!* I want to say, *She didn't overdo it, it was you! You grabbed her, that's why she stumbled.*

I take a step forward. Mum sees me.

'Lucy,' she says, and I stop. 'You should be in bed.'

Dad turns. Sees me. Smiles. 'We all should be in bed,' he says.

Now he's closing the dishwasher door and she's taking off her heels and he's locking up and she's turning off the lights and they are coming towards me. Because it's all over. Time for bed.

'Mum?' I say.

She gives me a little smile. There's a red mark on her forehead.

Dad's right behind her. 'We'll clean up this mess in the morning,' he says. He holds my eye.

And then they both wait for me to move. To lead the way upstairs. To go to bed.

Because it's all fine. Nothing really happened.

Really.

Nothing happened.

CHAPTER 5

Count the steps. Twenty-nine, thirty, thirty-one, and on up to the second floor.

I breathe faster. And faster. I'm at the door to my room on the third floor. My chest is tight. My brain spins.

Why does he do it?

I lower myself onto the chair.

He twists everything. It was *his* fault. Not hers. His. If he hadn't started the argument ... if he hadn't grabbed her ...

Keep breathing. It's okay.

But it's not okay. And it's not fair. He trips everyone in the room with his words, and the words he doesn't say are worse. Because you still hear them but you can't reply. *It's your fault, Alice ... Drawing is not a real talent, Lucy.*

All night, deep down, I knew a fight was coming. And the worst part is, there's nothing I could do to stop it.

I tilt my head back and count the ceiling panels. Four times six equals twenty-four. Twenty-four ceiling panels.

It wasn't always like this. It wasn't. Even when we first moved onto Millionaire Square three years ago, it wasn't this bad.

Like the day, almost a year ago, when I moved up here from my room on the second floor, and Mum said, *I just don't get it, those pokey old servant's rooms are practically in the attic.* But it was Dad, not Mum, who stood up for me. He said, *Ah, leave her to it, Alice. She's old enough to make up her own mind.*

My main wardrobe wouldn't fit up here because the ceiling is too low. So Dad took me to buy a new one. He didn't even look at the price, he just said, *You'll need a new bed to match that,* and he went to the mattress section.

Before I knew it, he'd jumped up on a bed and started bouncing on it. He made me do it too. But just as the manager came over, he jumped down. So I'm the one who got in trouble, while Dad wandered around the shop complaining loudly that parents are to blame for the behaviour of their kids. Which made me laugh. Which made the manager angry. Which got me kicked out. Which made Dad laugh until he cried.

And when he finally joined me in the car park, he had bought a desk and chair, and a full-length mirror too.

I mean, things have never been perfect between Mum and Dad. They fight. But all parents do. It's only gotten really bad since he bought The Old Mill eight months ago.

I'm looking directly above me now. Staring at the only

27

ceiling panel that matters. Because this room has something my massive room on the second floor didn't have. Something Mum and Dad don't know about. A place that's mine where their words can't reach.

I stand, slide the ceiling panel back and then lift myself up into the attic. I flick a switch, and the attic inhales the glow of the lamp.

Portraits are pinned to every rafter. Faces stare back at me. Mainly of Mum and Dad, but there are other people too. Megan, her parents, Ms Cusack, people I see outside of the window. Even myself.

It's not the eyes or the smiles or the worry lines that I'm trying to draw, but what's underneath.

There's a slight draught. It's coming from the other end of the attic. From Mr Reynolds's house. These houses are old and our road is actually one long terrace, which means we share a roof with Mr Reynolds. Dad loves that. But what he doesn't know is that we share an attic too. Up here, it's just one open tunnel that runs above every house.

Some of our neighbours use their space for storage. Ms Cusack stores books and clothes and paintings. Hazel's family has boxes of baby clothes, a high chair and old Christmas decorations. But mostly, the attics are covered in a layer of dust so thick that creeping through them is like crawling over the surface of the moon.

And for every house, there's a panel that can be lifted and tossed aside. If I wanted to, I could sneak into Mr Reynolds's house in the dead of the night. I could drop down into

Ms Cusack's and find out what she does in there all day. If I wanted to.

And Dad has no idea. Because he has never come up here. He doesn't know to look for it.

He has his secret. I have mine. Except I know about his.

'*Questionable,*' I whisper. The word flows through the cobwebbed stillness until it gets absorbed by the darkness further down where the dim lamplight can't reach. I love how sound gets soaked up in the attic, the same as in a forest. Everything is softer.

'*Illegal,*' I whisper. The word drowns in the space and it's quiet again.

'*Practical,*' I say. But the word doesn't hang on the air like it did in the cellar. Here, it dissolves and disappears.

That's the thing Mum doesn't understand. Even if there was no attic, I'd have moved up here. Because our house is filling up with words. But it will take them a long time to reach my room. Up here, it's quiet. And it's all mine.

SUNDAY

CHAPTER 6

I wake up to Mum getting into my bed like she always does in the morning and my first thought is, is Dad angry this morning?

She pulls the duvet up to her chin, her face inches from mine. She doesn't usually wear make-up at home. But she is now. It almost covers the red spot above her eyebrow.

'Morning, monkey,' she says. 'Thought I'd wake you while it's still summer.'

'Where's Dad?' I say.

'Downstairs,' she says. 'I'm making a pavlova today.'

It takes a second to figure out what she means. 'The dessert?'

'Yep.'

Oh, no. 'I wonder . . . will you burn it,' I say.

'And a salad,' she says.

'I wonder will you burn that too.'

Mum flicks me on the nose. 'I wonder will you regret mocking my glorious cooking when you see the feast I prepare.'

Mum made up the *I wonder* game because I hate getting out of bed. She crawls into my bed and wonders about all the great things that will happen during the day until I laugh.

But I don't feel like laughing. Because today I wonder what mood he's in. If he's said sorry. If they've made up. I look at the bump on Mum's forehead. 'Does it hurt?'

Mum scrunches up her eyebrows like she doesn't know what I mean. So I touch the bruise with my finger, but not hard.

She pulls back before catching herself and turning her grimace into a smile. 'Oh, that?' She runs her fingertips over it. 'Not really. But I wonder if I'll ever learn that high heels and champagne do *not* mix.'

I don't laugh. It's not funny. Because that's not what happened.

Where's Dad?

But she's staring at me, waiting, so I think of something funny to say. 'I wonder will Mr Reynolds clip his nose hair today.'

Mum laughs. 'It's awful, isn't it? I wonder if he has a hedge trimmer big enough. And a truck to carry it away after.'

I laugh because that's what she wants me to do. 'I'm starving,' I say. Jumping up, I run out of the room.

Downstairs, it's a new house. The windows are open and the tabletops gleam and the shelves are filled with freshly washed crystal glasses, and the smell of detergent has bullied any rising thoughts of last night back into hiding.

Dad's sitting on a stool in the kitchen. He doesn't see me. There's a full cup of coffee in front of him. He's leaning on his elbow with the bridge of his nose pinched between his thumb and finger. Cursing softly, he shakes his head, sighs, and then sits straight and lifts his coffee.

'Dad?'

He jerks a bit in surprise but then he smiles. 'Lucy!' He holds out his arm. 'Come here and give your old man a hug.' He's in a good mood, so they're probably not fighting any more. He holds his arm higher. His smile widens. So I go up and he hugs me, resting his head on mine. 'What's your plan for today?'

I'll probably draw. 'Nothing,' I say.

He's quiet for a second. Then, 'That sounds perfect. I'd do the same if I could. Enjoy your freedom while you can.'

I have a feeling he's talking about himself, not me. 'Work?' I say. 'It's Sunday.'

Dad takes his arm back and lifts his mug again. 'It sure is. And I get the pleasure of spending it on the golf course with a guy so lacking in ability that he'll probably have his shoes on the wrong feet.'

Mum comes into the kitchen behind me. She walks straight past us to the cupboard and takes out the granola. She fills a bowl and plonks it on the counter with some milk. Then she starts unloading the dishwasher.

I look at Dad. His coffee cup is half raised. He's watching

Mum. There are no creases clouding his face. It's like he's waiting to see what she'll do.

No one speaks. Dad takes a sip. For a while, the only sound is the stacking of plates and the clink of Dad's coffee cup. I'm almost through the whole bowl of granola by the time Dad says, 'How's your head?'

Mum puts a mug on a shelf. She holds it there a moment too long. But then she drops her hand. 'It's fine,' she says. She doesn't turn round. She goes back to the dishwasher and takes out the cutlery holder.

'Well, take it easy today, love, yeah?' Dad says.

Mum nods but doesn't turn.

'God, what I'd give to stay at home with you two today.' His words are like one of those *I'm sorry* cards with a picture of a sad dog on the front. Except that he's forgotten to write on it, or sign it.

Mum comes over and takes the coffee cup from his hand. 'Finished?'

'Thanks,' he says, letting her take it even though it's still half full.

The doorbell rings and I pretty much leap into the air and run down the hall. When I open the door, it's Megan. Her bike is locked to the lamp post. I totally forgot she was coming over today. Her pink hair is in two spiky pigtails. I've no idea how she convinced her parents to let her do that. She's wearing the shortest shorts known to man and a baggy T-shirt. I hadn't even noticed it's hot out today.

Her eyes squint a bit as she looks over my shoulder, down

our hallway, and I realize I'm just staring at her. 'Okay,' she says, like by not inviting her in, I've answered a question she didn't ask. She points behind her. 'I'll meet you at the park then.' She swivels around and follows her finger across the road.

I don't want to stay inside. I need air. Running to the kitchen, I tell Mum that I'll be in the park, and then I grab a sketch pad from its hiding place in the sitting room.

The park is right across the road from our house. It's pretty big for a city park. There's a playground at one end, a fountain in the middle, and loads of little gardens that are filled with flowers because it's summer. Bushes and trees line the whole thing, but you can still see the roofs of the Georgian terraces that surround it.

During the week the park gets busy, especially at lunchtime. This early on a Sunday, though, it's quiet. Still, Megan has managed to practically sit on top of three boys our age.

One of them is cute. Like, dimples and messy hair cute. Another is trying to play a guitar that seems way too big for him. He's cute too, but in a toothpaste-ad kind of way. I drop down beside Megan and whisper, 'Could you have sat any closer to them?'

She doesn't answer. Instead, she shuffles her bum an inch or two towards the boys and says, 'I might learn the guitar,' loud enough for half the park to hear.

I smile.

'What?' she asks.

'Will you sing too?'

'Of course.'

'Can you learn at home alone in a room where no one can hear you, please?'

'Nope.'

'I'm helping you,' I say. 'You don't want to be that loser that insists on singing and no one wants to tell them they're tone deaf. Trust me. I know. I'm tone deaf too.'

'At least you can draw,' she says. 'I wish I was good at something.'

'Drawing is not a real talent,' I say. The words slip out from somewhere inside before I can catch them.

'Yes it is!' she says but I cut her off.

'You're good at loads of things,' I say. 'You are amazing on violin.'

'But not good enough to get into the City Youth Orchestra.'

'Because you don't practise,' I say.

'Can't be *bothered* to practise,' she corrects.

'And your blog is brilliant,' I say. Her blog is called *Penny for Your Thoughts* and it's about a made-up girl called Penny who always gets in awkward situations.

'That's not a talent. That's just me messing.'

'Nah,' I say. 'It's definitely a talent.'

Megan shrugs. 'I'd prefer your talent,' she says.

'And you are good at jumping on trampolines,' I say. 'Remember your brother's birthday party last year? You bounced higher than all the six-year-olds there.'

'That's true,' Megan says. 'And I've really neat handwriting.'

'And you are great at covering school books in that sticky plastic stuff; I always get bubbles caught in mine. And your hair's the pinkest I've ever seen. And you're good at making friends. That's a real talent. A practical one. And it's good for me because I don't need to make loads of friends because you do it for me.'

I've managed to rob Megan of words, which is probably a talent in itself. She crashes sideways onto the grass like I've beaten her with too many compliments and closes her eyes against the sun.

After a while, she says, 'Yeah, well, they don't hang blog posts in museums.'

But imagining my portrait in the gallery doesn't make me feel proud. I shake my head and look towards my house.

They didn't fight again. That's good. So why does it feel wrong, like there's something I'm missing?

I see Hazel coming through the park gate. She's wearing shorts and a tube top and her curly hair has been straightened by a steamroller.

She comes over and sits down beside Megan. 'I'm so sick of being stuck inside practising all day.' She flips off her sandals and stretches her legs out until her feet are almost on my sketch pad. Orange tan streaks her ankles like dripping paint. 'I've hardly been out all summer. The Youth Orchestra is just . . .' She flicks her head. 'Just . . . urgh!'

'Check this out,' Megan says to Hazel.

Hazel waits as Megan leans backwards until she's in Guitar boy's face. 'Can I try?'

He looks confused and he hands the guitar out like she's holding a gun to his head. Megan takes it but holds it the wrong way round and I have to hide my smile.

'You need to . . .' he says, making a turning movement with his hand, but Megan pretends not to understand and Hazel laughs. The guy doesn't know what to do until Megan goes, 'Oh!' and flips the guitar over. Then she makes a shape with her hand and strums. 'Like this?'

The guy winces at the sound. 'Kind of.' He tries to show her where to put her fingers without getting too close but his hand shakes a little. She's making him nervous and I feel kind of sorry for him. Megan's always like this: the more awkward boys get, the more confident she gets.

I lean over and whisper so quietly, only she can hear, 'He fancies you.'

She nudges me away. 'Okay, like this?' she says and tries again. This time it's perfect.

He says something that could be, 'Yeah.'

Megan says to Hazel, 'Think I'm a natural.'

Hazel laughs. 'You are. You should have auditioned for the City Youth Orchestra on guitar!'

Megan holds out the guitar for the guy to take. 'I was only messing,' she says. 'I know violin and a bit of guitar, so I can do a few chords.' She doesn't look directly at him now though, which means she fancies him too.

'You *are* a natural, Megan,' Hazel says. 'I don't know why *I* got in and *you* didn't.'

Megan just shrugs. The thing is, though, Hazel's looking

40

at Megan, but you can tell her words are for everyone. Because she's saying Megan's good. But she's also saying she's better.

Am I the only one that notices stuff like that?

'There are *loads* of kids in the orchestra coming to The Green!' Hazel says.

The Green is short for St Cormac's on the Green, our new school.

'You're coming too, right?' Hazel says to me.

I nod.

'Do you know many other kids coming?' she asks.

'No.'

'Well, at least you know me and Megan, you can hang out with us,' she says and smiles, which is actually kind of nice of her.

'And we know everyone,' Megan says.

'Or will within a week,' Hazel says.

'Hey.' The voice is from behind Hazel. There's a girl around a year older than us standing there. Maybe it's the angle I have, but she's long. Long hair, long legs, long nose, long face. And she's wearing the same colour tan as Hazel.

'Oh, hi!' Hazel says, and jumps up.

'Did you forget I'd be over?' Before Hazel can answer, she says, 'Your mum said you'd be here.' Then she takes one look at the boys and lays a towel on the grass on the other side to them.

'This is Lisette, my cousin,' Hazel explains to me, sitting

41

back down beside Lisette. 'Lisette's already in The Green but she's in the year above us.'

Lisette waves at me. 'You'll love it, it's a blast!' she says and Hazel laughs like what she said was funny. Then Lisette whips off her T-shirt and lies down in her bikini top and shorts. A few seconds later, Hazel whips off hers too. Then she looks over at Megan as if she just asked her a question and is waiting for an answer.

'What?' Megan says.

'You don't want a tan?' Hazel asks.

Megan looks down at her oversized T-shirt. 'White's the new tanned,' she says.

'Suit yourself,' Hazel says. She starts to lie down but suddenly Lisette bolts upright, clutching her stomach. Her face scrunches up in pain and her hair falls around her like a half-closed hospital curtain. As Hazel watches her cousin, her own face scrunches up too.

'You okay?' Hazel asks.

'What's wrong?' Megan asks.

'Is it appendicitis?' I ask, half joking. I've had appendicitis and it's like a burning hot poker in your side.

Lisette does a fake laugh. 'Funny,' she says and, groaning, she holds her stomach as if it's a gaping wound. But she's like the hero at the end of a badly acted movie who's been shot and is trying to convince you she's going to die, but really everyone knows she's going to pull through. 'Just that time of the month,' she says.

'Oh,' I say.

Watching Lisette, it looks terrifying. But then her phone beeps and for a second the pain falls away from her face as she reads a message. Then, just as quickly, she's back clutching her side and moaning. I look at Megan to see if she has noticed, but she hasn't.

'You poor thing,' Hazel says. She looks at Megan. 'Trust me, it's a blessing you don't have it yet.' And again, it's there. That vanilla voice, spiked with thorns. Because she's pretending to be nice, but what she's really doing is letting Lisette know that Megan doesn't have her period.

'It's okay,' Lisette says and lies back again. 'It's passed. For now.'

Hazel shakes her head at the unfairness of it all.

'At least we're only five miles from the nearest hospital,' I whisper to Megan. I take out my phone and put it on the ground between us.

'We better ring ahead, let them know the severity of the situation,' Megan says.

'Tell them to stock up on more supplies,' I say. 'Gauzes and bandages and towels. Anything they can get their hands on.'

Megan bites her lip, but it doesn't stop a laugh coming out like a snort.

'What?' Hazel asks.

I'm about to make something up, but from behind us there's a yell and Megan turns to see what's going on, and in the next second a water balloon smashes straight into her chest. Another comes sailing over my head and bursts on the ground. Hazel and Lisette jump up to get away but I stay where

I am because when I turn, I see Guitar boy tackle another boy to the ground and pummel him with water balloons.

Megan's white T-shirt is soaked. I can clearly see her red bikini top beneath it before she holds the T-shirt off her body and wrings the water out. Hazel and Lisette check each other and then they sit back down.

'Such kids,' Lisette says.

'I know,' Hazel says. 'Why are we sitting near them?'

Megan hugs her knees in tight and pulls her T-shirt over them.

'Take it off, it'll dry in the sun,' Hazel says.

'It's fine,' Megan says.

But Hazel looks at Megan over her sunglasses. 'You've a bikini top on anyway, right?'

Megan doesn't answer.

'So just take the T-shirt off,' Hazel says.

Megan doesn't. Hazel raises her eyebrows and Megan opens her mouth. But for once, nothing comes out. Megan's eyes search the trees for some excuse, and it's so obvious why Megan doesn't want to take it off, but Hazel just keeps waiting.

'Here,' I say, and whip my top off. I've a string top on underneath anyway. 'You can wear this.'

I hand it to Megan and she tries to find a position where no one can see her and switches tops as fast as she can.

I'm right; she doesn't want anyone to see her in a bikini because she doesn't want anyone to know that she has nothing much to hide. Even though it's completely obvious,

44

Hazel is still saying, 'In this heat it'll dry in minutes,' and there's a smile in her voice, and you can just tell, she knows too.

The girls lie down. Megan reties her hair. No one speaks. Hazel plugs her earphones into her phone and gives one end to Lisette and one to herself. Then she taps her nail on the screen as they listen to music, and I think of the clink of Dad's coffee mug on the countertop this morning.

Mum and Dad didn't fight again. That's good. But they didn't talk about it either, they just pretended nothing had happened. Went back to normal. And that's the problem. Because if no one says anything, *normal* just becomes waiting for the next time.

Lisette removes the earphone and looks at Hazel.

'I'm still not talking to Stephen,' Lisette says.

'I don't blame you,' Hazel says. 'I don't know how you can sit next to him in Youth Orchestra. Too bad you can't move over to me at the other end of first row.'

'Yeah,' Lisette says. 'Too bad.'

They share pouty faces, and then Hazel asks me, 'You play anything?'

'No,' I say. You'd swear by her look that I've just said I sit in a dark room all day staring at the wall, so I add, 'I draw.'

'Oh, right, yeah, you won something?' Hazel says.

'Yeah, it was one of those competitions on the back of a Cornflakes box,' I say. Hazel thinks I'm serious. But Megan laughs. Then Lisette laughs. And just in case I don't know what laughing means, Lisette adds, 'You're funny.'

Hazel looks from me to Lisette, and when her eyes meet mine again, she's smiling. Maybe she just got the joke. Or maybe she's happy for me that Lisette thinks I'm funny.

'Megan writes a blog,' I say. I wait for Hazel to reply because she must know, she must have read it. But she stays quiet. 'It's really good.'

Hazel says, 'Mmmm.' Then she turns to Lisette. 'I doubt you've read it? Megan writes about her life.'

'No, I don't,' Megan says. 'Penny's made up.'

Hazel looks over her sunglasses at Megan. At Megan's shorts first, but then at her T-shirt, or, more specifically, at what the T-shirt is hiding. 'Parts of her definitely are anyway,' she says. Then she sits back like she said nothing.

I drag my eyes from her to Megan. But before I can make a face, Megan looks away. Again, she takes down one pigtail and reties it.

Is everyone just going to pretend that Hazel isn't doing this? I turn back to Hazel. 'Which parts?' I say.

'What?' Hazel says.

'Which parts of Penny are different to Megan?' I ask.

'Oh, I dunno,' Hazel says. 'I was just agreeing that Penny is not Megan. Anyway, I like the blog. It's cute. I keep a diary too.'

'It's not a diary,' Megan says.

'No,' Hazel says. 'I know.' And she closes her eyes. 'Are you going to forgive him?' I don't know what she means until she rolls on her side and faces Lisette.

'I don't know,' Lisette says. 'We were on a break, but it's not just that he kissed someone else, it's *who* he kissed. You know?'

46

'I know,' Hazel says really seriously, like one of those talk show hosts on daytime TV, and it annoys me so much that she can treat everything Lisette says as so important while putting Megan down every chance she gets, that I say, 'I had the same problem. I kissed a boy and fifteen minutes later, he kissed someone else.'

Lisette lifts herself up a little. Hazel watches me over her sunglasses.

'We were playing spin the bottle,' I add.

'Oh,' Lisette says and laughs. Then she holds her stomach and says, 'Stop. It hurts too much.' She wipes her eyes. 'You're funny!'

Hazel says, 'You *are* funny. We're having pizza at mine later, want to join?'

I look at Megan. Judging by her face, this is the first she's heard of a pizza party. And I think I'd rather hang out in a wasps' nest for the afternoon.

'Can't,' I say. 'Me and Megan are going out for lunch with my parents.'

Megan gives me a look like she's confused.

'Actually, we better go,' I say.

I stand. So does Megan. She can't seem to figure out what's going on, though, so I grab her hand and start walking.

'Where are we really going?' Megan whispers as soon as we're out of earshot.

'Anywhere they are not,' I say.

CHAPTER 7

We go out of the park and around the corner beside my house, onto the next street.

'So . . .' Megan says. 'What's wrong?'

Does she really not see it?

'Hazel,' I say.

'What about her?'

I stop walking. 'Is she always like that?'

'Only on Sundays,' she says.

'You're *funny*,' I say and she laughs. I grab my side. 'Don't make me laugh. It's that time of the month. You'll have to call 911.'

Megan pushes me off the path.

Megan doesn't talk about things that upset her. Not really. It's like the way you can sometimes see stars when you don't look directly at them. To get Megan to talk, it's better not to ask her straight out. But right now, I can't think of another way.

We walk slowly.

'Really, though, is she always like that?' I ask.

Megan looks at me and shrugs. 'What do you mean?'

'The way she talks to you.'

But Megan makes a face and I can't tell if she really doesn't know what I mean or if she'd rather pretend Hazel's doing nothing.

'I mean the way she . . .' But I don't finish because how do I explain? Do I say, 'Hazel was calling you flat-chested?' Because she didn't. She never actually said the words.

Megan is watching me, waiting.

'She just seems to make fun of you, or put you down, or something,' I say.

She lifts her eyebrows like she's considering it. 'Sometimes she tries to act more grown up when Lisette is around, that's all.'

But that's not it because she was doing it before Lisette arrived.

Megan starts walking again like it's all cleared up. But I don't move.

Maybe it's better that Megan doesn't get what Hazel is doing. Because I know how it feels when you hear the words people don't say. The words that hang around long after the ones that were spoken disappear.

She turns and looks surprised that I'm still standing here.

Or maybe she knows what Hazel is really saying, but finds it easier to pretend.

'Lucy, what?'

'Nothing,' I say.

She makes a *come on* gesture with her hand.

'I think I'll go home,' I say.

'Oh,' she says. 'Will I come with you?'

I shake my head.

Megan frowns. She looks over my shoulder at the park, then back to me, like she's saying, *So why did you make me leave?*

I open my mouth, but again I've no reply. So I turn away, and I know she's watching me, wondering what's going on, but I keep going.

I turn back onto my street. Ours is the first house, the one on the corner. The front door is unlocked. I lean my forehead against the frame and take a few breaths. Slowly, I count to ten.

I wonder what Mum is doing. Should I try to talk to her about what happened last night?

When I step inside, it's calm. Until I hear rapid footsteps going through Dad's office. A door slams. Fast feet on the stairs. He appears above me.

'Lucy. Where have you been?' Dad asks.

I feel like I've been caught doing something wrong.

He takes the steps two at a time. 'You,' he says. He grabs my arm. Holds something up. It's a Scrabble board. 'I was about to ring you. Golf got cancelled. Oly's here. I bet him a hundred quid you could beat him at Scrabble.'

He wraps an arm around my shoulder and escorts me down the hall. 'You're on my team.'

CHAPTER 8

It's roasting in the back garden. The branches of the bushes from Ms Cusack's house droop over the backyard wall and tickle Dad's head. He blows at them like he's blowing hair out of his eyes but they don't really move.

We've put up the umbrella for shade but it's still so hot that it's sticky.

Dad pushes aside the remains of Mum's salad and half-burned pavlova, and swigs his beer. It's me and Dad against Mum and Oly. Dad sinks his chin into his hands and stares at our letters. 'Vowels. Bloody vowels.'

A black cat slinks along the wall, dodging leaves. He must belong to Ms Cusack. He looks down at me with this expression like even he thinks we've no chance of winning. Then he drops into Ms Cusack's garden.

'Only one bloody consonant,' Dad says.

The game's nearly over and we're losing. And,

unfortunately, we have three A's, two U's, one I and an N. Fortunately, however, we're not playing the usual rules.

'I've got a word,' I say. I lift the three A's and place them after another A on the board. Then I add the two U's. So my word is Aaaauu.

Dad sticks his chin out like Popeye and squints. 'Aaaauu?'

Oly lifts his eyebrows in doubt. 'Go on, explain.'

'Okay,' I say. 'It's like the sound an ambulance makes when it roars past, the way the tone changes? Except this is the sound a person makes when they are screaming because they are running away from lava.'

Dad sits back, swigs his beer. 'Yeah, that works.'

'Not worth a lot, though,' I say.

Dad makes his *I beg to differ* face. 'I beg to differ,' he says. 'You got rid of our vowels. You hit a double word score. And you made up a fabulous new word that doubles our score again. I'd say that was a success.' Then he stares at Mum and Oly, like he's daring them to disagree.

These are the rules me and Dad invented when I was little. It's the same as normal Scrabble except you can make up words. They can't just be gibberish, though, they have to resemble real words. And this one is pushing it. Mum and Oly now both have their eyebrows raised and they are just waiting for the other to object. I better give them something more.

'I know all the two-letter words, right?' I say.

Mum nods. So does Dad. 'Because she's a genius,' Dad says, tapping the table. 'Sorry, go on.' He gestures for me to continue.

'Well, Aa is the name of a lava that flows fast.'

Oly doesn't look convinced.

'Check it,' Dad says.

Oly grabs the Scrabble dictionary from the middle of the table to look it up. And I'm correct.

'So, if Aa is a real word,' I say, 'then I think the sound you make when you are running away from it should contain the word.'

'Exactly,' Dad says. 'And it's onomato-thingy.'

'I think we better allow it,' Oly says.

'Damn right you better,' Dad says, but he's messing. Well, kind of. *In this house we play to win.*

Mum nods. The red mark on her forehead is turning purple. I try not to look at it.

'Twenty-four points,' Dad says and high-fives me. Then he picks out our letters as Mum and Oly mumble to each other about their next word. There's no time limit, so Scrabble can take hours in our house. Which is okay by me on a day like today when the sun is shining and Dad's happy.

'Oh, for the love of ...' Dad says as he places our new letters on the tile rack. 'What are we supposed to do with four Ns? And that's the last of the letters.'

He swats at the branch, which swings high and then falls back to tickle Dad again. He hates Ms Cusack's bushes spilling into our garden. One day last summer, he hopped over the wall and chopped them all back. By evening her garden looked like a bad haircut, with shaved patches between the clumps. In the morning there was a letter in our post box telling Dad never to enter her property

53

again. Dad declared that that was the last time we did her any favours.

He was only trying to help. But maybe she got scared or something. I know I would if I was living alone and a strange man came into my garden.

'Has anyone ever been into Ms Cusack's house?' I ask.

Dad barks a laugh and Mum looks up at him from under her eyebrows, and her smile says she knows something about Ms Cusack, but it also says that Mum and Dad have made up.

Mum nods at Dad to tell him to explain. Dad sits back and plays with the label of his beer as he thinks. 'I went in there, all nice, when we first arrived. Thought I'd make friends, so I brought a hundred euro bottle of tawny port with me. The second I stepped in, though, I wanted to turn and run. I felt like a kid entering a witch's house.' He leans forward and whispers like he's scared she'll hear. 'There are these masks on the walls, I swear to God, the eyes follow you around, like some voodoo thing.'

Mum's smiling and shaking her head. Oly's drinking up his words.

'There were ancient newspapers everywhere and they were soaked in . . .' His eyes dart to the wall. 'Let's just say she has a lot of cats.'

'Disgusting,' Oly says. 'I hate cats.'

'And the furniture? It's like the little shop of horrors. I doubt anything has ever been washed. I was afraid to sit down. Not that I got the chance.' Dad wears his scared face and he starts shaking his whole body. 'I'm standing in her hall, stammering like a school boy, *Myself and my family have moved in next door, I wanted to say hello*, when she just goes crazy!' Now Dad waves his arms in the air. 'She starts shrieking about us *suits* taking over her street. Next thing, she grabs the bottle of port from my hands, opens it, takes a swig, and pushes me out the door!'

'She did not!' Oly says.

'She most certainly did. *Crazy*,' Dad says, relaxing back into his chair again. 'Think there's a few screws loose there. And not just from old age.'

'Loose screws is right,' Oly says. 'I've heard a story or two.'

'Oly!' Mum says like she's scolding him.

'I asked around because we were interested in that house,' Oly says.

Dad nods to back up the story, and Oly goes on. 'Apparently she used to live in Paris.' Then he leans in. 'Burlesque dancer, I heard. And seems she brought her love of dance and a good party back with her.' Oly winks, which always gives me the creeps. 'Wild lady,' he mouths.

'But I've never seen anyone go in there,' I say.

Oly shakes his head like he doesn't care; he's not changing his story.

'Does she ever go out?' I ask. 'How does she get food?'

Oly looks at Dad. Dad shrugs. And Mum is busy studying her Scrabble pieces.

'Does she have any money, Dad?' I say.

'I doubt it. But that would be her own fault,' Dad says. 'She's sitting on a property worth over two million and she probably only uses the bottom floor. The upper floors are rotten, no doubt.' Dad wags a finger at me. 'I'd give her one point five million in the morning. She could spend her remaining years splashing out on a luxury cruise liner if she wanted to, rather than wasting them as a penniless artist, watching that dilapidated shack fall down around her.' He shakes his head.

I blink. 'An artist?'

'Yeah, she's a painter or some nonsense like that. Probably never done a decent day's work in her life. I just don't understand the choices people make. Imagine, no husband, no money, just a crumbling house full of useless paintings that no one's ever going to buy. Hobbies are one thing. But choices that impact your whole life? And your neighbours' lives? There are mistakes and there are *mistakes*.' He swigs his beer.

'Wait, got one,' Mum says and Dad's eyes jump to the board.

Ms Cusack's a painter?

Mum puts down the word Jetty, with the J on the triple letter.

'Thirty-eight points,' Oly says. 'Great score this late in the game. Any luck with those four N's, Declan?' And Oly smiles like they've won.

I try to shake Ms Cusack from my head. Instead, I look at our letters. NNNNGUI. I count up the scores. We're forty-two points behind and they've only two letters left. I can do this. I'll show him I can.

'There's nowhere left to go,' Dad says. 'Unless we play off that O.' He runs his tongue over his teeth.

I look at the letters again. Then the board.

And I have it.

'*Nunning*,' I say. 'It's what you do all day when you are a nun. That's eight points. Doubled because it's made up. And an extra fifty because we used up all our letters. And the two points for *No*.'

Dad sits back and looks at me with eyes as wide as the sky. 'Genius. Bloody genius.' He holds up his hand for a high-five and I slap it as hard as I can. Then he grabs me in a headlock and rubs his knuckles into my head. It hurts but I'm laughing. 'That's what I'm talking about. Winner!' Then he lets go and turns to Oly. 'Do not even pretend you can do anything with those two vowels you've left, Oly. Looks like you owe me a hundred.'

Oly takes out his wallet. He doesn't hand the money to Dad, though. He hands it to me. 'She earned it,' he says.

Dad laughs. 'Tell you what, take these leftovers inside and you can have my half of the money, love.'

I smile. And pocket the money.

I clear the food and when I'm standing in the kitchen, I whisper the word *Nunning*. It flies through the air and explodes like a firework and a thousand little *nunnings* drift lazily to the ground. It's a real word now.

The fridge is brimming over with food. I have to push everything around to make room for the leftovers. Uneaten salmon platters and just-in-case salami trays and buy-one-throw-one-out meals. Half the food we buy gets chucked in the bin. No one would even notice if it went missing.

And I imagine an old-fashioned fridge, empty and smelling of sour milk in this heat.

She's a painter.

Before I know it, I'm taking out one of the three packets of bacon on the shelf. A block of butter. Two yoghurts, a bunch of bananas, a tub of tomato soup, a box of eggs.

I go to the cabinet. Tins of beans and peas and tomato sauces. I pile them on the counter. From the next, I grab pasta, rice and instant noodles. And from the fruit bowl, I pick apples, oranges and a mango.

When the pile is so tall that it's spilling over, I run to the cellar and grab an empty wine box and come back and fill it with all the food. Then I take it down the hall and out the front. Down my steps. Over to next door. Up the steps. I drop it in front of the door. I look around. No one's watching. Her curtains are closed.

But she's at home. She has to be. She's always home.

Last time we do her any favours. But I want to. Just in case she needs it.

I lean forward, ring the bell, and then turn and run back home. And as I step inside, the breeze that comes with me carries a rush of happiness with it. But then Dad appears in the doorway to the kitchen and the breeze scurries away.

He saw me. He knows what I did.

Everything was going so well. He was happy. He was having fun. I was a *bloody genius*.

'Lucy,' he says. 'We're on a winning streak. Grab the Monopoly board.' Then he's gone, back to Mum and Oly.

I have to hold the banisters for a few seconds before I push myself upstairs to get the board.

MONDAY

CHAPTER 9

'Here, shove over,' Mum says the next morning. She lifts my duvet and the mattress sinks as she gets in beside me. 'I wonder if it'll stay sunny all week,' she says.

I groan.

'Come on,' she says and nudges me.

'What time is it?' I ask.

'Time to get up,' she says.

'That's not a time.'

Mum sighs. 'It's almost eleven.'

'Fine,' I say. 'I wonder . . .'

He made us play every board game in the house last night. We ended with Monopoly again, double or quits. But I was on Dad's team so we won. In the end, we made three hundred and fifty euro, and I got about seventeen high-fives from Dad. And he let me keep the money.

'I wonder . . .' I say again. I wonder how I convinced myself that the fights are all his fault. They're not. People argue. And anyway, it's not him, it's the stress. Once he sells The Old Mill, everything will be fine.

'I wonder will I find the smart-yet-funky suit I really want to buy today,' Mum says. 'I wonder will it make me look smart-yet-ten-years-younger.'

'Why do you want a suit?'

'I don't have one.'

'So?'

'So, what if I needed one? Summer sales are on, so I thought, why not?'

I wonder does Dad really mean it, that Ms Cusack deserves to be alone and poor. And I wonder if she brought the box in. She hadn't by the time I went to bed.

'Nothing?' Mum says.

'I wonder what Ms Cusack does in there all day.'

'Ooh, good one,' she says. 'I wonder does she have a painting worth millions just lying around.'

'I wonder is she sad.'

Mum chews this over. 'Yeah, I wonder that too.'

The drawing I made of her, the one that won the competition, was of an old woman sitting on a threadbare couch, twirling her thumbs like she was spinning time.

'I wonder does she regret becoming an artist,' I say.

Mum turns to me. 'I wonder is it the best thing she ever did?' Her face is so close to mine, I feel the stir of her eyelashes as she blinks. She waits for me to respond.

'Even if it was a mistake?' I ask.

She takes her time responding. 'If we avoided mistakes, we'd never try anything, would we?'

I don't have to wonder if Dad agrees. I know the answer. *Some things shouldn't be tried.* But I don't want to think about it any more, so I say, 'I wonder what we'll eat today.'

Mum looks at the ceiling. She sighs again. 'A burrito.'

'I wonder what you have against Pablito's Burritos,' I say.

'I wonder what they have against wiping down tables,' Mum says. Then she rolls out of my bed. 'Fifteen minutes, then we're out the door. You can bring Megan if you want.' She goes out of the room.

Megan. I forgot about Megan. Grabbing my phone from beside my bed, I text her.

Me
Hey. Sorry about running off yesterday.

I tap my phone with my thumb as I wait. Megan doesn't reply instantly, and Megan *always* replies instantly.

I try another tack.

Me
Want to come shopping with me and Mum?

I should have texted her last night. Or called. Said sorry. But I kind of forgot all about it. Between board games, I kept sneaking out to check the box of food. I wanted Ms Cusack to take it in, so she'd have it. But I also didn't

63

want Dad to see it out there if he went to the Local or something.

The Local is the private members' club where he and Oly and Mr Reynolds and everyone else involved in development in the country go to make deals. It's next door to Mr Reynolds and it's another reason why Dad wanted to live on this street.

My phone beeps.

Megan
I'll be there in twenty.

She's not mad at me! Whoop! I hop out of bed and get dressed. But before I run downstairs, I open my window and stick my head out.

The box is gone!

I really hope that means that Ms Cusack took it inside and not that someone robbed it during the night.

Paula is in the kitchen sweeping when I come in.

'Morning,' I say.

'Well, good morning. There's granola on the table,' she says.

I want to complain that I'm tired of granola, but Paula will scold me for being spoilt. *The world is filled with starving people.* So instead, I shove a dry handful in my mouth and put on toast. I get the jam from the cabinet. We've three, four, five different kinds, and that's not including marmalade. Jam's going in the box next time. But I'll do it in the morning just after Dad leaves for work.

Did Ms Cusack stare at the box for a long time, wondering who left it? Is she in there now having bacon and eggs for breakfast?

I chew another handful and look through the window at her bushes. It's strange how two houses could look like each other from the outside but be so different inside. 'I wonder if Ms Cusack is lonely.'

Paula stops sweeping. 'Who?'

'Ms Cusack.'

'As in, Ms Cusack next door?'

'Yeah.'

Paula purses her lips like she's thinking about it. Then she goes back to sweeping. But I can't get her falling-down house out of my head.

'She must be lonely,' I say.

'Why?' Paula asks.

'Because she's alone and no one ever goes in there and she never goes out.'

She stands straight again and studies me.

'What makes you think she doesn't go out?'

'Because I've never seen her,' I say.

'What makes you think no one goes in?'

'Because I've never seen anyone go in,' I say.

Paula shakes her head at me like I'm strange and goes back to sweeping.

My toast pops.

'Dad says her house is a state.'

'Does he now?' She jabs the floor with the brush like she's

annoyed. Maybe she doesn't like me saying Ms Cusack's house is dirty.

'I didn't mean it like that,' I say. 'I just meant, maybe she needs help or something. He says there are newspapers soaked in cat pee covering the floor.'

Paula attacks the fridge with the brush, trying to get as far beneath it as possible.

'Dad says she has a few screws loose.'

'Oh, for God's sake,' Paula says and leaves the room.

I think I might have upset Paula.

But she comes right back into the kitchen and leans the brush against the countertop and glances at the closed door to the family room. Mum must be in there. She comes closer.

'What happened to your mother's forehead?'

My toast is going cold. I pick up the knife and start buttering it. 'They were arguing,' I say, 'on Saturday after the party, and she tripped. But it was an accident.'

Paula's eyes are burning a hole in my head but I don't look up. I'm saved by the doorbell. I run to answer, still holding my toast, and then, for the second day in a row, I stare at Megan. This time, though, it's because I don't know how to explain what happened yesterday.

'Mum dropped me off,' Megan says and grabs the toast from my hand and shoves it in her mouth. 'So . . .' she says, sliding her phone out, 'I have . . .' She makes a drum roll sound and crumbs fly everywhere. 'One hundred and eighty-three *likes*.'

Her blog. It's got to be.

Mum comes out behind me. 'Ready?'

'Hi, Mrs—' Megan starts but Mum holds up a finger, like she always does. 'Alice,' she says.

'Hi, *Alice*,' Megan says.

'Good morning, Megan.'

'Mum,' I say, 'I'm not ready. I'm starving.'

'So get up before noon one of these days,' Mum says and pulls the door closed behind us.

'It's not even noon now,' I say.

'Well, it will be by the time you eat,' she says.

Megan holds out the end of the toast. 'Want this? I'm stuffed. Had a huge breakfast.' She grins and I stick my tongue out.

'We'll get you something in town,' Mum says.

When we walk past Ms Cusack's, I see something on her doorstep.

I wait until Mum's a few steps ahead and I dash up to her front door. An old book! Sticking out of the book is a note. I slide it out.

Food for the mind ... A fair exchange, no?

It's for me. I know it is. I glance toward Megan. She's about to ask me what I'm up to, so I put my finger to my lips to tell her to stay quiet and then shove the book down the back of my jeans.

'What was that about?' Megan whispers when I get back to her.

'I'll tell you later,' I say.

She gives me wide eyes, like she can't wait, but then Mum turns to see what's going on and Megan holds her phone up high, like she was having trouble finding signal.

'Ooooh,' she says, 'one hundred and eighty-four *likes*.'

I know she's pretending, to cover for me, but still, Megan is slightly obsessed with how many *likes* her blogs get. She'll spend the whole day checking.

'When you get to two hundred, can you swap them for something real, like an egg sandwich?' I ask.

'So why didn't you make one?' Mum says, completely missing what I said. 'There are loads of eggs in the fridge.'

Actually, there are not. Not any more. But I don't tell her that.

'Did you write a new blog?' I ask.

Megan studied writing at summer camp for three weeks. She already had the blog but now it's more popular because everyone from camp shares her posts.

'Yup,' Megan says. 'It's called *Penny in the Park*.'

I grab her phone and read as we walk.

Penny meets three boys in the park. One has a guitar. By the way they talk, you'd swear Penny was going to marry Guitar boy. But then Penny's T-shirt goes see-through after she gets hit by a water balloon and the boys get an eyeful of Penny's massive boobs.

It's funny. But . . .

'It's good,' I say and wobble the phone in front of her face.

She puts it in her pocket. 'Thanks,' she says.

Something feels off about it, but I can't figure out what yet, so I say, 'Aren't you worried that they'll read it?'

'Who?'

'The boys from the park.'

'They'll never see it, will they? It's just friends who read it,' Megan says. 'Girls. The others on the course.'

'It'll be fine, then,' I say, flashing a smile.

Fine because she can't get caught just *bending* the truth. Pretending.

That's it. That's what's off about it. I mean, I get that Penny is made up. But she's not, really, is she? She's basically Megan but with the bits she doesn't like removed, and other bits added. Like Megan's life, just made better.

We cut through the university in the middle of the city, but Mum stops to look at her phone. 'Actually, while I'm here ...' she says. She makes a call, chats for a second, then hangs up. 'I'm just going to pop over there and meet someone.' She points to a building with doors the size of a double-decker bus. Then she rummages in her bag and hands me a twenty. 'I'll be a few minutes. Well, let's say thirty minutes. You can grab food at that café.' She nods over my shoulder at a small coffee shop beside a grassy area with a few tables and chairs outside.

She starts to leave but then turns back. 'Wait for me on the grass if you finish early, okay?' she says. 'No wandering.'

We watch Mum cross the stone courtyard. Now that she's gone, I feel awkward again. Like I should explain to Megan what yesterday was about. But before I can figure out what

69

to say, Megan asks, 'Want to go check out fake nose rings on George's Street?'

'Sure,' I say. 'But I'm grabbing a sausage roll first.'

As we go into the café, I slide the book out from the band of my jeans. *To Kill a Mockingbird*.

'What were you doing on your neighbour's doorstep?'

I tell her about the box of food. When I look up, Megan is giving me this weird look.

'What?' I say.

'You gave her extra food from your house? Why?'

'Dad said she's a penniless artist. I was worried that she doesn't have money for food. And I think I'm right because maybe she gave me this book as a way of paying for it.'

'You're ...' Megan looks at the ceiling above the food counter. 'What's the word? Oh, yeah. Nice. You're a nice person.'

I finally have some food in my stomach, so we walk out under the main entrance arch of the university. It's busy. There are tons of tourists taking photos and shoppers rushing past and a homeless guy writing in chalk on the ground:

Don't look down on others. I am a writer, a poet, a joker, a friend, a loser, a lover, an optimist, a nihilist, a man. I don't need pity, I need a helping hand. If you can't spare some change, spare a kind word.

I watch him fix one of the words that got smudged. He has

a shaved head and a scar on his face, but there's something soft about him too. He doesn't even have a home or money for food, but he's still saying he'd feel better if people were just nice to him. Talked to him. I thought I was being nice to Ms Cusack. But maybe if I was really nice, I wouldn't have left the food there and run away. I'd have stayed to talk to her.

Beside me, a girl says, 'Spare change?' to someone walking past. She adds, more to herself than the person who ignored her, '. . . for the train.'

She has brown hair like mine. Maybe a year older. 'Train to where?' I ask her.

She looks surprised. 'Anywhere,' she says. 'Once I'm on it, I can stay on all day.'

I grab a fiver from my pocket and hand it to her.

'Thanks,' she says. And she hands me something. It's a piece of paper with a message. *I hope you feel safe all day*. I turn it over, but that's all it is. A wish in neat handwriting.

When I look up, the girl has moved on, and I place the note into the cover of the book beside Ms Cusack's note.

As I catch up with Megan, she's slipping her phone back into her pocket.

'Well?' I say. 'How many *likes*?' I'm teasing and I immediately feel bad because I know it matters to her. 'I'm sorry. About yesterday, I mean.'

She gives me an awkward smile and looks away as quick.

'It's just, I don't think Hazel is always nice to you,' I say.

'Don't worry about me. Or Hazel. Sometimes she just

71

gets in these moods. Next time we see her, it'll be different, I promise.'

I'm pretty sure that means she knows what I'm talking about. But I don't push it, because her admitting that much is enough for now. Instead, I say, 'Things are a bit weird at home.'

Immediately, she's looking right at me. Because she's never awkward once she can focus on someone else. 'What's wrong?' she asks.

'They don't fight all the time. But he gets into moods, you know? Because he's stressed. On Saturday they argued and she tripped.'

We turn off the street into an outdoor market that sells clothes and books and jewellery.

'The bruise over her eye?' Megan asks.

So she noticed. I nod.

We stop by a nose ring stall and look at the fake studs.

'Are they arguing a lot?' she asks.

'More since he bought this big new development.' I think of the twenty-two million he owes, but I'm not supposed to know about that, so I say, 'Parents fight, right? Do yours fight a lot?'

'Once or twice a year, maybe,' she says.

Oh.

She holds a ring up and looks in the mirror. But she's not looking at her reflection. She's looking at mine.

'Once or twice a week,' I say.

And before she drops her eyes, I see the surprise in them. She plays with another fake nose ring, one of the round

72

ones with a ball on it, before meeting my eye. 'Has she ever tripped before?'

'No,' I say.

I hold her stare until she finally nods.

She picks up the one with the ball on the ring again and puts it under her nose. 'What do you think?'

'You look like a bull.'

'I like it,' she says.

'Of course you do,' I say.

'I bet you like the tiny studs,' she says.

'So?'

'So, you can hardly see them, what's the point?' she says.

'That *is* the point,' I say.

But Megan shakes her head. 'You're a quiet person. You need to wear things that are loud so they do the talking for you.'

'And what does a bull ring say?'

'That you're tough.'

But I don't think I agree. If you have to wear something to show people you're tough, then you're probably not.

Behind the stall there's a girl sitting on a stool looking nervous and there's a tattooed guy kneeling in front of her with a hole puncher up the girl's nose. He doesn't say, *Ready*, or anything. He just squeezes it and it goes *clunk* and tears start streaming out of the girl's eyes.

'I'm not crying. It's just my eyes are streaming,' she says.

'I think that's the definition of crying,' Megan whispers. Then she wanders to the next stall.

While her back is turned, I buy two fake nose rings, and when I catch up to Megan, I hand hers out, saying, 'So the world knows how tough you are.' But what I'm really saying is, *sorry about yesterday.* I'm saying *thanks* too, but I'm not sure what for.

She slips it on and smiles with all her teeth. Then she takes her phone out and reads, and slowly, her smile is wiped away.

'What?' I ask.

'Someone left a comment on my blog.'

CHAPTER 10

Megan shows me her phone. It says,

Yes, I'm sure they were all absolutely shocked by what is under your T-shirt, Penny. Sorry, I mean, isn't under there.

And somehow I know it's Hazel.

Megan takes the phone back. She looks at me for a second like a flower that's wilted but then she turns and goes out of the market. I run to catch up.

'Megan?'

'It doesn't matter,' she says and shoves her phone in her pocket like that'll make the comment go away. 'It's just an anonymous comment.'

No, it's not anonymous.

'Exactly,' I say. 'You've a hundred and eighty-four likes.'

'A hundred and ninety now,' she says. Megan slows a

bit. I'm not going to speak until she does so I know what she's thinking.

She doesn't talk until we pass under the arch. 'She spread a rumour about me once.'

'Who?'

'Hazel,' she says, which means she's admitting, in a Megan kind of way, that she also thinks Hazel wrote that comment.

We cross the courtyard and sit down on the grass.

'She said I was anorexic and that's why I've small boobs.'

'What? When?'

'Two months ago. Online.'

'Why didn't you tell me?'

Megan shrugs. I know what she's saying. She didn't want to make a big deal out of it. But by the way she's hunching her shoulders, I have a feeling she's just as upset about *what* Hazel said as why she said it.

'She somehow always manages to point out to people that I've no boobs. Like the time she told everyone in orchestra that *Double A bras really do exist. That's what you wear, right, Megan?*'

I can't believe Hazel did that.

Actually, I can.

'I'm small too, Megan,' I say.

'I know,' Megan says.

'And, Megan,' I say, 'I don't care.'

Megan doesn't say that she doesn't care either. Because she does. She picks some daisies and starts making a chain. 'She told me that it wasn't her that spread the anorexia rumour but that she was worried about me because I looked sick. She said she would, *support me any way she could.'*

'She said that?' Spreading a rumour is bad enough, but then pretending to be the supportive friend is a whole new level of horrible.

Megan doesn't go on. She just picks daisies.

Even though it's summer, the campus is busy. I look at the building Mum went into. She should be coming out soon.

Megan places the daisy chain on my head. I smile but she's already back to picking more daisies and I don't want to make her talk if she doesn't want to. So I take out *To Kill a Mockingbird*.

Does Ms Cusack know it was me who left the food? Why did she choose this book? I'm about to start reading the first chapter when the note the girl gave me falls out.

I hope you feel safe all day

All day. All.

Not *I hope you feel safe today* or *I hope you always feel safe*. But *all day*, as if feeling safe for some of the day is the best she can usually get.

I imagine her sitting on the train, watching the houses and the sea whizz past. Eating half-finished sandwiches left on seats. Reading the free newspapers they hand out. Counting the number of people in her carriage or the amount of times she passes through Pearse Street train station.

Did things get bad for her at home until it got to the point where being on the train is the best part of her day? Was it something big or did all the little things slowly build up?

And I think of Mum's bruise and Ms Cusack's empty fridge and the nasty comment on Megan's blog.

I hope you feel safe all day. There's a whole life in that word: All.

Mum is coming out of the building. I stick the book into my jeans. She's with a man. She turns and gives him a hug. Then comes skipping down the steps and he stays there and waves goodbye.

'Who's he?' I ask when she reaches us.

She turns around to see but he's gone. 'No one,' she says.

I give her a look, so Mum says, 'Just an old friend from when I went here. He lectures now. We were catching up. Shall we?' and she starts to walk towards the arch.

Megan grabs my arm. 'Who is he?' she whispers.

I shake my head. 'I don't know.'

'Is *he* why they were arguing?'

'No!' I say. That's ridiculous.

Isn't it?

CHAPTER 11

Megan had to go home after shopping because she's visiting her cousins until tomorrow night, and I'm dying to read *To Kill a Mockingbird*. Dad's still at work, so as soon as we get back, I go straight up to the attic. But now that I'm here, I remember something. There's a painting in Ms Cusack's attic. It never occurred to me before, but maybe, if she really is an artist, she painted it?

There's an ancient wooden chest in her attic, pushed into the space where the sloping roof meets the floor. I pull it out a bit and open it. Inside is the purple suede jacket with white fur around the collar and a thick belt. Beneath is a pair of flared trousers. The jacket's too big but I put it on anyway.

I know what's in every chest and box, I've searched through them all before. Flowing clothes with floral prints. Old newspapers. Books with titles I don't recognize. But resting against the roof is the painting with a sheet draped over it. Pushing aside cobwebs as thick as fleece, I crawl over and slide the sheet off.

It's an oil painting of a man on his knee, proposing to a woman, with a look in his eyes that says he loves her. It's good, the painting. So good that I almost feel like I know who the man is. It belongs in a museum.

It's hard to see in this light and I squint as I search the rough oil surface. But then I see it, there's a signature in the corner. *D. Cusack*! She *did* paint this!

The woman in the picture has long flowing hair to match a long flowing skirt. She's turning away from the man and she has the strangest look on her face. Like she wants to be somewhere else. I trace her outline with my finger. Why did Ms Cusack put it in the attic if she painted it? She could sell it, get some money. Maybe she's forgotten about it. After all, it looks like years and years since anyone came up here.

Then I remember the words, *She's a spinster, through and through.*

Is this a self-portrait? Did Ms Cusack once turn down the man in the painting and later regret it? Is that why it's up here, because she couldn't bear to have it on her wall, the reminder of the mistake she'd made?

I picture her handwriting, spidery and sprawling, on the little note inside the book she gave me. *Food for the mind.* I wonder what the book is about and if she's trying to tell me something.

Still wearing her jacket, I hurry back, and sitting down on my beanbag in my attic, I open the first page.

*

Mum's putting a lasagne in the oven when I come down later.

'What are you reading?' she asks, pointing her chin at the book in my hands.

'To Kill a Mockingbird,' I say. 'It's good. It's about a girl called Scout whose father is a lawyer defending a black man accused of hurting a white woman.'

I grab a sketch pad and go into the conservatory.

I think the accused man is innocent. Maybe Ms Cusack's trying to show me that good people get accused of bad things because they are poor or because they are different. Or maybe she's saying that people need to stand up for others, like Scout's father stands up for the black man.

I start to draw Ms Cusack, but this time, she's younger. Her long hair falls over her face as she sits at a kitchen table, reading. The room is messy and a fly noses an empty milk carton beside the sink.

Mum wanders through from the kitchen with two glasses of orange juice. Sitting down beside me, she slides over *To Kill a Mockingbird*. 'Haven't read this in years,' she says and opens it, one hand lifting some juice while the other holds the page open.

I watch the faraway look come over Mum's face. It's like the faraway look on the woman in the painting in Ms Cusack's attic. It's not happy. It's not sad. It's somewhere else.

I draw the younger Ms Cusack, her hand following the words she's reading. The other, however, holds the last page that she read. It's torn out and scrunched up in a ball, held above a steaming mug of hot water like she's about to dunk it in. I add another scrunched-up page to her mouth.

81

Mum leans over. She looks at my drawing but doesn't ask.

After spending ages on her face, I draw a fridge behind her, the door left open with nothing inside. Then I make it night-time by putting a candle on the table and shading out everything but the woman and the words and the fridge and the mess.

Beside me, Mum turns a page.

Back on the woman's face, I try to get the faraway look just right. After a while, I smell burning.

'Mum?'

'Yeah?'

'The lasagne?'

Mum jumps up and runs to the oven. 'It's okay,' she calls and I hear her curse quietly as she puts it down on the countertop.

She comes back in, wiping her hands with a tea towel. 'Just a little crispy on top,' she says. Which means it's probably cremated.

Standing above me, she looks at my drawing as she drains her juice.

'The title is, *Food for thought*,' I say. 'She's a woman that devours books.'

Mum coughs suddenly and sprays juice everywhere. Even on my drawing, which makes me laugh. Now she's trying to apologize but she's half-choking, half-laughing. She starts dabbing my drawing with the tea towel. 'I'm so sorry! My juice went down the wrong way! I just wasn't expecting you to say that,' she finally manages. 'But that's funny, *devours books*.'

'I thought so,' I say.

Mum keeps dabbing at my drawing.

'It's fine, it'll dry,' I say and move it across the table until it's sitting in a patch of evening sun. 'It'll probably look good when it dries, it'll have that old, crumpled look. Besides, covering the page in juice suits the theme.'

Mum barks another laugh and dries her eyes with the tea towel. 'Where did we get you from? You're too smart for me.' She shakes her head. 'Right, dinner.'

I follow Mum into the kitchen and grab plates to set the table in the conservatory. Mum is cutting the lasagne into squares when we hear the front door opening. She looks up. 'Your father's home,' she says. A second later it slams. Mum holds the knife in the air.

If he calls out, it means he's in a good mood. We listen. There are footsteps on the stairs. Nothing else. And the silence from the hall swoops in and collects around us, like a mist turning to rain.

Mum cuts more lasagne. I hide my drawing and bring the salad to the table. By the time he arrives, the food is ready. He grabs a beer from the fridge and sits down.

'Idiots,' he says.

Mum doesn't ask who he means but her shoulders get a bit stiffer. She keeps sneaking looks at him, like she can't tell if it's better to speak to him or stay quiet. She gives him two slices of lasagne and before she even sits, he's shovelling it in like he's been too busy to eat all day. I cut mine up into tiny pieces so it looks like I'm eating, but Mum doesn't even do that.

Dad points his fork at Mum's plate.

'It's the heat,' she says. 'Never hungry when it's hot.' She eats a little anyway, though. Then he looks at me, so I start eating too.

No one says anything for ages. We're so quiet that a bird hops in through the open conservatory door. It pecks at the floor, then stops and cocks its head, looking straight at Dad as if waiting to hear what he'll say, too. Then it flies back into the garden, and I think of the animals that can sense earthquakes before they hit.

Dad shakes his head. 'Everyone is tied up until September.' He says, *tied up*, like you might say *lying*. He takes another mouthful and chews.

And I know it means he hasn't gotten any more investors for developing The Old Mill, which really means that he hasn't been able to find money to pay off Mr Reynolds.

'Oh. That's a shame,' Mum says. I wish I could warn her, tell her to be careful. She doesn't know about the twenty-two million.

'Yeah,' Dad says, 'it is.'

Mum eats some more. Dad takes a third slice. He's almost finished when Mum says, 'But there's no rush.' She says it in the voice she used to use when she was trying to coax our old cat out from under the bed. 'September's fine.' She smiles. 'Don't let it get to you.'

And even before he replies, I hear his words revving up inside him. I put my fork down.

'Alice,' Dad says and shakes his head. 'I don't think you understand how this works.'

Mum takes the tiniest bit of food. She doesn't meet Dad's glare. He reaches over the table for a toothpick and then starts rummaging around in his mouth.

'Well, what did you do today?' he says to me.

I stop myself from glancing at my sketch pad on the shelf and I try to think of something practical. But there's nothing. Instead, I remember the girl who was asking for money for the train. 'We went into town this morning. There was this girl asking for money for the train. I gave her some and she gave me a piece of paper that had a wish on it.'

I'm about to explain what I mean when I see Mum's face and I remember what she said when she left us at the café. About staying put. I think of a quick lie. 'She came over to us when you were in that building catching up with—'

'Anne,' Mum interrupts. I look at her because, well, it's not true, but she's too busy giving Dad a fake smile. 'I met Anne for a coffee. She rang this morning.' Mum blows out air and her lips flap like a deflating balloon. 'I immediately regretted picking up the phone. She was having a meltdown over Kevin. He won't commit, blah, blah, blah.' She makes this rolling motion with her hand to show how Anne goes on and on. She takes a sip of water. Then she starts nodding like mad, as if Dad said something that she's agreeing with. 'But she's not giving him a chance either.'

Dad scratches his cheek and watches Mum.

She doesn't look at me.

'I don't understand why you keep running around after that woman,' Dad finally says. 'She sabotages every relationship she has, including her friendships.' He gives Mum some time to think about this. 'And every time she rings, you just drop everything and run.'

Mum sighs. 'I don't drop everything and run.'

She's getting into an argument over something she didn't even do!

'She's using you,' Dad says. 'It's always the same. As soon as she has a problem, she's all over you.'

'She's always there for me when *I* have a problem.'

'Really? Give me one example?' Dad says.

Mum sucks in air like she's about to reply, but she doesn't.

'Right,' Dad says, 'that's what I thought.'

Mum takes a deep breath. 'Look, I just popped into town for half an hour for a chat. It was better than letting her come here, she would have stayed all day.'

'I don't want that woman in our home.'

Mum shakes her head like she has no idea what to say any more.

'I'm serious,' he says.

'Oh, I know you're serious,' Mum says. She clatters the empty plates together and lifts them but she doesn't walk away.

'Which means?' he says.

She drops the plates back down on the table. 'Which means, you don't get to pick my friends for me.'

'I do,' Dad says, 'if you're not capable of picking suitable friends.'

Mum slaps the table. Everything rattles. 'No, Declan, you do *not* have the right to decide who I can be friends with.'

'So you get to decide who comes into this house?' Dad laughs like it's ridiculous. 'I don't have the right to protect my daughter? You just make all the rules,' he says.

Their words are curdling the air. I stand up. Gently, I push my chair back. Step towards the kitchen. He doesn't notice me. He only sees her.

And creeping away, I know I'm leaving her alone to battle it out on the bottom of the ocean. But I can't stay.

I can't stand it.

Up in my attic, I lie on the floor in the dark, breathing out their words and breathing in the stillness.

It'll stop soon. It has to. I mean, Mum doesn't know about the twenty-two million. Once he gets the money and flips the mill, he won't owe anything and he won't be stressed and it'll go back to what it used to be like, before Dad turned my playroom into his wine cellar and spent all that money on bottles he never drinks, and joined all those clubs with private membership, and bought more properties than he can count, and started spending money like life is a game of Monopoly.

It'll be fine.

TUESDAY

CHAPTER 12

I'm tired. Last night I read Ms Cusack's book for hours before I finally fell asleep. Now it's morning but Mum doesn't come in and wonder about things with me today.

When I go downstairs, I catch a glimpse of her slipping out of the front door. She's all dressed up in the suit she bought yesterday. She closes the door. I have no idea where she's going. Or who she's going to see. But I bet it's not Anne.

There's granola in a bowl. Again. I sit at the marble countertop and pick at it.

Paula comes in with a basket of ironing. She stops and looks at me. Then she puts the basket on the floor, fills the kettle, and sits opposite me.

'What happened?'

'They had a fight, last night.'

By the way she's nodding, I think she knows anyway. I swear Paula can taste the air in this house. 'I'm sorry, Lucy,' she says. 'I know it's hard when people fight. And when it's your parents, it's even harder.'

'Did you fight with your husband?'

Paula blows out air.

'I mean, when you were still married,' I add.

She nods. 'After a while we couldn't remember why we were arguing any more.' She stands and gets a glass of juice. She places it in front of me but keeps holding it until I look up. 'You know, they say *failed marriage*, but plenty of good things come to an end. And plenty of bad things go on far too long. To me, a failed marriage is one that continues after it's gone bad.'

The kettle boils. She fills the teapot and sits down again, and as she's pouring tea for herself, the front door opens. Feet stomp down the hall and Dad appears in the doorway. He leans against the frame. 'Well, hello! How are we all this morning?'

He's never here during the day. Why is he home? And where's Mum? I hope he doesn't ask.

'Where's your mother?'

I look at Paula.

'She went out before you got up,' she says to me, like I was the one who asked. And something about the way she lifts her teacup and blows on her tea says she doesn't know where Mum is because it's none of her business.

In the doorway, Dad shifts his weight a little and coughs. 'Right, well, I just forgot something, so I'll grab that . . .'

Paula keeps sipping her tea so Dad looks at me instead.

"You, young lady, should get out and enjoy the sunshine. Beautiful day!'

Then he spins round and goes to the stairs. I can tell he's taking them two at a time.

'I think he's in a better mood,' I say.

'Oh, goodie,' Paula says. But then she winks at me, which makes me laugh. I think Paula is the only person in the world who doesn't care what mood Dad's in.

'I'm just going to . . .' I nod towards the door. I want to know why he's in a good mood, did something happen with The Old Mill?

Paula nods as if to say, *off you go*.

I climb the stairs quietly. He's whistling. His footsteps are already coming towards the landing. He appears at the top, holding a folder. His phone rings. 'Oly!' Dad says. 'Good news! We're on! Ten solid ones off Seanie. The money should be in my account by this evening . . .'

I stand still as millions of little *questionables* crawl like ants out of every hole and crevice. But this is good news, right? He got the money, so it's all going to be fine.

'. . . well, what can I say, when I'm good, I'm good.'

He grins as he passes and pretends to rugby tackle me. I step aside.

He pauses by the front door, hand on the knob, listening to whatever Oly is saying. 'Well, as soon as that money is in my account, I'll transfer it to Reynolds. Then I'll personally head down to Planning, see if we can't get this mill flipped ASAP. Right, talk later.'

Dad waves over his shoulder at me, then steps outside and slams the door shut on all the little *questionables* trying to slip out with him.

He said the money should be in his account by this evening. He's going to pay back his loan to Mr Reynolds. That's good, right?

CHAPTER 13

I'm still standing on the stairs when my phone beeps.

Megan
I'm outside.

That's weird. She didn't say she was coming over. And why didn't she just ring the bell?

I go down and open the door. For a second, she's silhouetted by the brightness of the day outside. But as soon as she steps inside, I can see that she's about as happy as a cornered mouse. She holds out her phone.

It's the comments section of her blog.

> That wasn't water from a balloon. It's because Penny
> peed herself laughing at some pathetic joke she'd

just made. Eek! Embarrassing because NO ONE else was laughing. And the smell matched the whiff of desperation that poured out of her as she practically begged the boys to like her.

Some friendly advice, Penny. You're not funny. Those boys were laughing at you, not with you.

Wow. No wonder she's so upset.

'Should I delete it?' she asks.

'Yes, of course!'

'I mean the blog,' she says, and wilts against the wall. 'There's no point in deleting the comment. I tried. It goes straight back up again under another name.'

'You can't delete the blog, Megan,' I say.

I hear Paula come up the hall behind me. I make an excuse and drag Megan upstairs.

'School starts in less than two weeks,' I whisper when we are on the first floor. 'If it is Hazel, and you delete the blog, she'll get at you another way, just like the other rumour she spread. You have to do something, Megan.'

She stops and looks at me like she's waiting for me to tell her what to do.

'Stand up to her,' I say.

'By doing what? She's not going to admit it's her. Same as the other rumour.'

'There's got to be something.'

But Megan's eyes start to glisten with tears. 'It's not fair,' she says. 'Everyone can read what she's saying.' And I know that, for Megan, that's just as bad as Hazel's words. Megan drags herself up the stairs again.

I follow her, but slower, because I'm hoping I'll think of something. But what can you do when you can't prove it's Hazel?

When I get to my room, Megan is staring at the ceiling.

'Lucy?' she says.

I follow her eyes.

The panel. I left it open last night. 'Wait—' I say. But I sound like an injured bird or something, which only makes Megan jump up on the back of the chair and stick her head into the attic. My attic.

'Lucy . . . ?'

I even left the lamp on.

'What is this?'

'It's . . .' But there is nothing I can say to stop her from pulling herself up.

She's above me but I can't see her face. Her back is to me. She's looking at my drawings. I feel a little dizzy, like she's rummaging around in my brain and reading my thoughts.

I wait. She doesn't move or call down to me, so I give in, and go up to her.

She stands like she's on a stage with a crowd of people staring back at her. Except the crowd is mainly made up of my mum, dad and Ms Cusack. And some of her own face, which she must think is weird.

It's like watching someone watch a movie. Her face keeps changing. She's amazed, impressed, freaked out, even a bit

97

disappointed, probably because I've been keeping this a secret. But one look settles on her face which is softer than the others, harder to read.

I follow where she's looking. It's Dad's face, the day he used a picture I'd drawn for him to light a BBQ because me and Mum made fun of him in front of some of his friends. At first, he laughed, but after, when no one else was watching, he gave me that *look*. Like I'd gone too far. Disappointed him.

Megan chews her lip as she jumps from Dad to Dad to Dad. Finally, when she speaks, her voice matches her expression. 'He looks so angry,' she says. She turns to me. 'Have they argued again?' she asks, but what she's really asking is, *Is there something you're not telling me?*

I don't want her here, I don't want her seeing these. Because somehow, it makes it more real.

When I don't reply, she asks, 'Bad?'

I shrug and try to sound casual. 'Same as usual.'

'About what?'

Dad's money trouble. Mum's fake visit with Anne. I don't really know. I don't even think they know.

'It's fine, Megan. It'll get better now that things have changed for Dad with work,' I don't tell her what things. I just hold her eye, hoping she will agree with me. Because it *will* get better. It has to.

Megan nods slowly and then looks at all the pictures. 'They're good, Lucy. Actually, they're amazing.' But now I turn my eyes to the floor until eventually she gets that I don't want to talk about them any more.

'How far does it go?'

When I look up, she's squinting into the shadows. 'All the way to the end of the row,' I say.

'Have you been down there?'

I nod.

'Any cool stuff?'

'No,' I say. 'No dead bodies or treasure maps.'

Please don't go down there. Please just forget about all of this and leave.

'Who else knows about this?' she says.

'No one,' I say, and I crouch on the floor like I'm about to drop back into my room. But she stays where she is, looking like she's doing maths in her head. 'What, Megan?' I say.

'Do all the houses have ceiling panels that open?'

'Why?'

'Just wondering,' she says. But then she speaks in this high-pitched, nasally voice. *'I keep a diary, too.'* The grin in her voice makes my heart quicken.

'Megan? What?'

She walks through Ms Cusack's attic.

'Megan, don't . . .'

She doesn't answer and I don't want her snooping on her own, so I snatch the torch off the floor and go after her.

By the time I catch up, she's almost halfway through the row of attics. She's not even looking around, she's just going straight ahead like she's on a mission.

'Megan, stop!' I say.

This time, she does. The torchlight catches her face and

she has that look again, like she's calculating something. 'Which one is hers?' she asks.

'Whose?'

'Hazel's.'

'Why?' I ask.

'I just want to know.'

But I get a feeling it's more than that. 'Why?'

'Because.'

'Megan!'

'Lucy, please? Come on? Look, I know my way around her house, I've been in it a million times. Right below that panel is the room where she practises violin. Her bedroom's below that. And she's at orchestra practice. And her parents are in work. And her sister's probably out. And she keeps a diary, too, Lucy. Remember?'

'What are you talking about? We're not going in there!' I say. That's got to be illegal, right?

'Just for a sec,' she says.

'Megan! If we get caught—'

'We won't.'

'But if we do . . . and anyway, what's the point?'

'To find her diary.'

'Her diary?'

'Yeah.'

'No way. We are not reading her diary, Megan.'

'You said I should do something!'

'Not that.'

'Why?'

Why? Because that's like Megan walking around up here, window shopping in my brain. Except worse. 'Reading her diary is like stealing her thoughts or something.'

'So what am I supposed to do?'

'Ask her to her face.'

'But she'll deny it. And I've no way of proving it's her.' Megan starts speaking in the nasally voice again. *'Penny's peed herself laughing at some pathetic joke she's just—'*

'I know, Megan, but . . .'

Megan grabs my hand. 'Please, Lucy. I just want to know. To see it written down by her own hand that it's her leaving those comments.'

'What difference will it make?' I ask. 'You still can't go up to her and say, *I know it's you, I read your diary.'*

'But at least I'll know, Lucy,' she says. 'When she's wandering around school with Lisette making fun of me, at least I won't feel like a complete fool.' She's pleading with eyes that glisten, but not with tears. Now they sparkle with the possibility of having a way of knowing for sure it's Hazel. And I sigh. Because I get it, there's power in knowing.

Besides, I won't be able to stop her now.

'Two doors down,' I say.

Megan springs forward and hugs me. Then she turns for Hazel's attic.

CHAPTER 14

Megan sticks her head down into what looks like Hazel's practice room. Then she turns to me. She looks like an action girl from a Japanese cartoon.

'It's empty. So, what's the best way down?'

'Megan!' I say. I don't even want to break in, now she wants me to take charge?

'I'm not good with heights,' she says. 'And you're used to jumping out of the attic.'

'My *own* attic,' I say. But she gives me her puppy-dog eyes. 'Fine.' Almost directly below us is a music stand holding some pages. In the corner is a chair. I can move that for Megan to land on.

I lower myself as slowly as I can and when my arms start wobbling from the weight of my body, I fall through and drop onto the floor with a thud. I really hope there's no one in the room below.

I tiptoe to the chair, and then get it into position. 'Come on,' I say.

Megan looks scared.

'Then don't do it,' I say.

But Megan's face disappears and her legs come through, and then with a jerk she drops down a bit. She hangs there. And shrieks.

'Shhhh,' I say. I hop up on the chair and wrap my arms around her flailing legs. She puts a hand on my head. Then suddenly I'm holding all her weight while her other hand is slapping my face. 'Megan! I can't see. Ow!' I think one of her fingers is up my nose. 'Stop, wait, take your hand—'

But Megan wiggles and I can't hold her any more. Or myself. I tilt back and the wall tilts forward and the chair topples over onto the floor and I land with a clatter with Megan on top of me.

Ouch. And oooops.

'Get off,' I say, pushing her away. There's no way we haven't been heard. I turn the chair and jump up and am lifting myself into the attic when, from below, Megan says, 'It's fine.'

I strain my neck to look. She's rubbing her head and looking out of the window. 'Stefanie's sunbathing. With earphones in. And no top on. Gross.' She turns back to me. 'It's fine. Come on.'

'What if there's someone else home?' I say.

'There won't be,' she says.

'But what if . . .'

Megan has her mobile out. She dials a number and somewhere far below us, I hear a phone. No one answers after fifteen rings. Megan hangs up. I'm still dangling here. 'Why didn't you do that five minutes ago?'

Megan shrugs. 'Didn't think of it. Come on,' she says and goes to the door.

I shake my head, take a deep breath, and lower myself again.

She's already halfway down the stairs by the time I get to her. It's so weird creeping through a house the exact same as yours, but not. Like you're snooping on yourself.

Hazel's room is on the second floor. It's really tidy. There are tons of golden violin awards all lined up in a row on her shelf.

One wall is covered with photos, normal ones and orchestra ones, but a photo of Hazel and Lisette with their arms wrapped around each other's shoulders is the biggest. It's beside her bed but tilted a tiny bit so it faces the door.

'Urgh,' I whisper. 'Is she always this . . .' I look around the room for the word. 'Organized?'

Megan looks under the pillows for Hazel's diary and I go straight to the window to keep an eye on Stefanie. As long as I can see Hazel's sister sunbathing in the back garden, we're safe.

Megan's looking under the bed. She's not very good at this.

I run to the bedside table and open the little drawer. Placed perfectly in the centre is a purple notebook with the words *Hazel's Diary* printed in neat writing on the front.

It's not right. To open it. To read it. It would be like

someone taking my drawings from the attic and taping them to the front of my house for everyone to see.

But Megan's beside me now. She grabs it and sits down on the bed and starts reading. I go back to the window.

Megan flicks through it, reading out dates and sentences at random.

I keep my eyes on Stefanie. She doesn't move a muscle. Maybe she's had a stroke and is dead.

'She's saying I'm immature,' Megan says.

'You are,' I say.

This wasn't a good idea. Besides the fact that Hazel's diary is private, what if Megan reads more horrible comments? She'll feel even worse.

'Hey, listen to this, *I was supposed to go to the cinema with Megan, but Lisette's staying over and if we went, Megan would just embarrass me, buying candy necklaces and eating them off her neck.*' Megan lowers the diary. 'She's the one that used to do that!'

'Megan, that's not why we're here. We're only looking for proof that Hazel wrote those comments. Just read the last few pages,' I say.

'Okay, okay.'

My skin's crawling. We're going to get caught, I know it. 'Megan, come on, let's go.'

She giggles like she just found some gossip. 'I think *someone's* a little paranoid,' she says.

'Megan, you're supposed to—'

'Listen,' she says and starts reading. '*I was taking out my* lunch when I saw Lisette staring at me, and I realized no one brings food, they just have Diet Coke, so really quickly, I said, "Poor Mum, she has no clue," and I dumped the sandwiches into the bin. Thank God no one else noticed, they already think I'm a kid, which is stupid because I'm really mature for my age, even Lisette says so. I'm not wearing anything tight until I can buy a padded bra.'

Wait . . . seriously? A padded bra? After that look she gave Megan in the park?

Megan reads another entry. 'Stephen is madly in love with Lisette. He texts her every night before he goes to sleep and first thing in the morning. Like he can't live without her for a second. I wish I had a boyfriend like that. Stephen is so perfect.'

'She likes Stephen!' she whispers. She flicks the page again. 'This is so good. She thinks he's the handsomest guy in the whole wide world. Seriously, she says that. Then Megan's eyes dart to the door. 'What was that?'

I don't hear anything, but I look out of the window anyway.

Stefanie's gone.

And now I hear singing.

I run out to the landing and I stick my head over the stairs but then whip it back just as fast. Stefanie's coming. She's on the flight below.

The singing stops. Has she heard us? She'll call the police. We'll be arrested. Dad will go ballistic. I risk a look again. She has earphones in and she's scrolling through her phone.

Where is Megan?!

I sprint back to her just as she's sliding the drawer closed. I pull her out of the room.

We rush across the landing and are just out of sight of the lower stairs, when, 'Hello?' Stefanie calls.

She's heard us. I wince. But I squeeze Megan's arm and we tiptoe upstairs.

'Hazel, you better not be trying to freak me out.'

We keep going, step by painfully slow step until we're at the top. We disappear behind the corner.

'Hazel! Aren't you supposed to be at practice?'

I push Megan to move faster. We creep along the top floor and slip into the practice room. Stefanie's running up the stairs now.

'Go!' I say.

Megan leaps onto the chair beside the music stand and lifts herself through the open ceiling panel. And gets stuck there. 'Lucy, help!' she says.

I jump up, take her feet, and throw her upwards as hard as I can.

'Hazel?' Stefanie calls.

Stefanie is just outside in the hallway. I leap high. Then Megan is pulling me and I'm kicking the air trying to pull myself up. And I'm inside.

We both kneel and lift the corners of the panel and slide it back into place and carefully let go. And just as the gap disappears, I see Stefanie come into the room.

I hold my breath and don't move a muscle. Ten seconds pass. Twenty.

Below, she moves again.

It's quiet. She's gone.

In the dark, Megan's panting. 'I got them! The last few pages!' she says, and her phone lights up. She took photos. Megan catches her breath, then whisper-reads.

Dear diary,

So much has happened.

I'M MADLY IN LOVE WITH STEPHEN HICKEY.

I know it's wrong but I can't help it. Here's what happened.

On Thursday night he texted me the violin maker's phone number. He said that the guy only makes the best, and that's what I needed, the best violin for the best violinist. Me! The best violinist!!!!!!!!!

Then on Saturday he offered to walk me to the shop. I didn't tell Lisette. We spent all afternoon together. It was amazing. He's so smart but so sensitive too. He knows EVERYTHING about violins. He seemed really sad when he talked about Lisette. He was sorry about what happened but he said Lisette is too self-absorbed and he's right, she is. He says being with Lisette can be really hard, and I know what he means.

He walked me home and the minute he left me, I started getting texts from him, saying don't worry, we'll get you a violin as special as you. And that, by next year, I'd be the one in first chair, which is where Lisette sits now, right next to him!

All day Sunday I was with Lisette, talking about whether she should forgive him . . . it was horrible! I was so afraid she'd use my phone and read my texts or something, but I couldn't make myself delete them.

Stephen is the most amazing boy. I can't even explain it. He's so smart and so cute.

I feel fantastic and terrible all at once.

Lisette just doesn't understand him the way I do.

'Oh. My. God,' Megan says. 'That whole time on Sunday she was persuading Lisette to get back with Stephen when she likes him!'

Megan is delighted. But I feel as uneasy as when I hear the front door slam and I'm waiting to see what mood Dad's in. Like there's a nest of baby snakes twisting around inside me.

We shouldn't know this. It's not fair. It's Hazel's secret

'Wait . . . Here it is . . .' Megan says. *'Megan's clueless. And that blog is so immature. I don't know who is more annoying, Megan or Penny. It's hilarious, though, because she deletes my comments but I just put them back up. I seriously have to ditch her before school starts, I don't need her embarrassing me.'*

Megan looks at me with *you see* eyes.

Okay. Now I don't know what to think. We shouldn't be reading this . . . but not only is Hazel leaving the comments, she thinks it's hilarious too?

Maybe she does deserve to have her secrets known, at least by Megan.

In the light from her phone, Megan's face glows and

109

her hair is a pink halo. She doesn't look crushed. Actually she loks like she's about to burst out laughing. Like the comments don't have the power to hurt her any more.

And I picture Hazel on Sunday, copying every expression Lisette made. Wearing the same clothes, the same hairstyle, the same fake tan. She wants to sit where Lisette sits. She wants to go out with Stephen. Hazel wants to *be* Lisette. And she thinks *Megan* is immature? 'What kind of an idiot is she?'

Megan's smile bursts free. 'Obviously the kind that understands him in a way Lisette never could.'

'The kind that wears a push-up bra,' I say.

'The kind that will be sitting in Lisette's chair next year,' Megan says.

'The kind that keeps a diary,' I say. 'In her bedside locker. Stupid hiding place.'

And then I have to put my hand over Megan's mouth because she's laughing so loud.

CHAPTER 15

'Lisette is going to find out that Hazel likes Stephen,' Megan says as she drains a glass of milk after we eat lunch in my kitchen. She pours another and dunks a cookie in it.

I'm clearing the food away, and I shove a jar of jam aside and it makes me think of Ms Cusack. There are six jars in total there now. Seriously. No one even likes apricot in our house. I lift it out and take a sliced pan from the bread bin. 'Let's go to the park,' I say and head for the front door.

'Are you still hungry?' Megan asks.

'Nope, they're for Ms Cusack,' I say.

When we get to Ms Cusack's door, I don't ring the bell.

'What's wrong?' Megan says.

'What if she answers and asks us to come in? Dad says the floor is covered in pee-soaked newspapers,' I say.

Megan steps back.

'Not her own pee,' I say. 'Her cats'.'

111

'Oh,' Megan says. 'Still, though. Gross.'

The red paint on the door is peeling so badly that older green paint sticks out in patches from beneath. I feel bad for her. I really do. But I don't want to go in there. I put the jam and bread down by the door and walk away. If Ms Cusack hasn't taken them in by the time we leave the park, I'll ring the bell. Besides, I might catch a glimpse of her collecting it.

Megan spots Guitar boy as soon as we're through the gate, and she goes straight over. He's with the cute dimpled boy. I'd rather keep an eye on Ms Cusack's front door than try to talk to two boys that I hardly know.

'I hope you've been practising the chords I showed you?' Megan calls out as we get close. Guitar boy looks up and goes red when he sees her, but he smiles too. She plonks down beside the two boys so I don't have much choice but to join.

'Have you been playing long?' Megan asks Guitar boy.

He looks at her like she just asked him to list every town in the country in alphabetical order. Eventually he manages to say, 'No. Just started.' For a second, he stares at her, but then he adds, 'You? I mean, the violin? Not guitar. Because I remember you said you play violin.'

'Yeah. My mum made me take lessons until a few months ago. But I just get bored, you know?'

Guitar guy nods around twelve times, and his eyebrows get more and more knotted as he searches the sky above Megan's head for something to say. Then the knots smooth out and he points at the other guy. 'Cian kite-surfs,' he says and sits back like he just unloaded a boulder. I've no idea what kite-surfing is but I don't want to ask in case I'm supposed to know.

'I'm learning, yeah,' Cian says.

'That's like surfing while holding a kite, right?' Megan says.

'Yeah, kinda,' he says.

Oh. That sounds cool.

'Lucy draws,' she tells them. 'She won the Young Artist of the Year Award. Her portrait is hanging in the gallery.'

'I came second,' I correct her, but Megan waves that away like it doesn't matter.

'There's a portrait of you in the gallery?' Cian asks.

'No, not me, it's of Ms Cusack,' I say.

'Who's Ms Cusack?' Cian asks.

'Her neighbour,' Megan says and points across the park at her house. A tree half-blocks the view so I can't see if she's taken the food.

Now I have to explain. 'It's what I imagine she looks like.'

'Why are you so interested in her all of a sudden?' Megan asks. Then she says to the guys, 'She's been leaving food on her doorstep.' She turns back to me and hands me silence like a present I didn't want.

'It's just . . .' They all watch me. 'Well, she grew up on this street. She must have had friends and family. She was probably happy. And now . . .' I shrug because I don't want to explain about her being an artist and what my dad thinks of artists. So I just say, 'Now she's alone. And poor.'

'See,' Megan says and points at me. 'Nice person.'

But there's something not right about what I'm saying.

Because that might be the truth. I do feel bad that she's poor. But I also want to know *why* she's poor. And lonely. And if she really deserves it just for becoming an artist.

'Hey,' Megan says. Her tone has changed, her voice has a secret in it now. 'Look!' She raises her eyebrows in the direction of the park gate. I follow her gaze. It's Hazel, with her head stuck in her phone, texting.

And immediately, the baby snakes in my stomach churn at the thought of Hazel's secrets. But then I picture Megan on the doorstep this morning. Wilted. Hazel did that. Now Megan has a glint in her eye and a smile on her lips.

And it's not like we're going to tell anyone her secrets anyway.

'I wonder who she's texting,' Megan whispers. '*Your new violin will be as special as you.*'

And I can't help but join in. 'The curves as smooth as your freckled skin.'

'The strings as tight as your straightened hair,' Megan says.

'The wood as orange as your natural tan,' I say.

'The sound as sweet as your nasally voice,' she says.

Megan turns so her back is to me. Over her shoulder she whispers, 'No one understands you like I do,' and then she wraps her arms around herself and rubs her hands up and down her waist pretending to be Hazel kissing Stephen.

The boys don't know what we're talking about but they laugh because Megan looks ridiculous.

Hazel lowers her phone and catches my eye. For a second

114

you can tell she wants to turn round, but then she decides to come say *hi*.

She walks over and sits down between the guys and says, 'What's up?'

'Where's Lisette?' I ask.

Hazel shrugs. 'Left her after practice.' Then she turns to Guitar boy. 'I've been flat out practising since yesterday.'

Megan points to the guitar. 'Can I?'

Guitar guy nods. He doesn't even go red this time.

Megan strums a few chords badly. She hums along and it takes me a minute to realize she's humming that tune they play when a bride walks up the aisle, and before I can stop myself, I'm laughing.

Hazel is still talking. 'The idea that talent comes naturally is a myth, I mean, you really have to put the work in too, don't you?' she says, which is kind of the opposite of what she said last time, about Megan deserving to be in the orchestra because she's a natural.

'Didn't you say you're getting a new violin, Hazel?' Megan says.

Now I'm not laughing. I'm nearly choking. I throw Megan a look but she doesn't see.

'Eh, yeah, I am.'

'Will it be special?' Megan asks. I try to kick her because she's going too far, but I don't want Hazel to see, so it's just a tap and she ignores me.

'Well, I'm having it made to order, so, yeah,' she says.

Megan can hardly hide her grin. Hazel's stare bores into her.

And then I can see the moment that Hazel realizes Megan is laughing at her, that she's missing something. She searches Megan's face a second more, then she says, 'I read your blog.'

The words are a grenade with the pin pulled, placed gently on the grass between us.

'It's funny,' she says.

Megan's head goes completely pink. I think she may just explode with the pressure of not being able to say the words, *I know it's you leaving the comments.*

But there's something about Hazel's smile. I've seen that smile recently. On Mr Reynolds. On Dad. 'Have you guys read it?' she asks the boys. 'Megan's funny. Sorry, I mean, *Penny* is funny.' Hazel clicks her phone a few times and I before I can cut her off with something, anything, she starts reading.

'*Penny in the Park,*' she says.

'Don't,' Megan says, but Hazel shakes her head as if she thinks Megan is being modest and keeps going.

And it's like at home, when the room shrinks and the air gets stolen away and you know what's going to happen but you can't stop it. Hazel's reading and the guys are listening and Megan's looking at Hazel like her brain hasn't caught up with what is happening yet. Then Guitar boy realizes it's him in the blog and Megan's face just freezes. He catches Cian's eye for a second and then they both look away.

The trees get closer and the park gets smaller and it's just us with these words churning between us.

Hazel reads, '*His fingers touch mine as he shows me a chord.*'

Hazel reaches out and puts a hand on Megan's arm like she's saying, *so good*. Like Megan is having as much fun as her. But Megan's not blinking and Hazel keeps going and Megan's eyes are begging Hazel to stop.

'I love this part,' Hazel says and reads the section where everyone sees Penny's massive boobs. The boys cough in embarrassment. Megan makes this tiny sound, like a mouse caught in a trap.

Hazel reads to the end, drops the phone and finishes with a loud, steady clap. 'It's really funny, right?' she asks no one in particular. She reaches over and touches Megan's knee. 'Honestly,' she says. She gives her an encouraging smile. Then the smile warps like plastic in a fire, into one of concern. 'What's wrong?'

Megan is a statue.

'Is it the comments?'

Oh, no, don't. Please don't.

'Someone's been leaving horrible comments. She just needs to ignore them,' Hazel says, but she's not even looking at Megan now. Her hand is on Megan's knee, but she's looking at Guitar boy. And she's lifting her phone again.

I have to do something to stop her. Even though I know I shouldn't, I say, 'How's Stephen?'

Her eyes dart to mine as she holds the phone in the air. I glare right back at her.

She shrugs. Her eyes go back to her phone.

'You like him,' I say. I'm not supposed to know. But I'll lie, say I saw them in the park or something.

But now it's Hazel that doesn't blink. 'No, that's Lisette.' And then she reads. '*Yes, I'm sure they were all absolutely shocked by what is under your T-shirt, Penny. Sorry, I mean, isn't under there,*' Hazel drops the phone. Shakes her head. 'Tell Megan she should just ignore that stuff.' And she actually stares at Guitar boy until he says, 'Yeah.'

'Your blog is brilliant, Megan,' Hazel says and gives Megan's leg a little tap. 'So funny.' Then she sits straight. 'I better go practise again. Our concert is in three days and I've a solo and I'm so not ready for it. I'm going to destroy it!'

Her smile is an invitation for one of us to tell her that she'll be great. No one speaks.

I'm in shock. I can't say anything. How can she be so cruel?

She stands and goes towards the fence. Guitar boy, Cian and Megan look anywhere but at each other.

And Hazel's just going to waltz away.

In the next second, I'm jumping up and running after her. 'You knew!' I call.

She's at the gate when she turns. 'What are you talking about?'

'You knew those were the guys from Sunday, Hazel, don't pretend you didn't know!'

'Megan's blog is made up,' she says. '*Penny isn't real.*' And her eyes twinkle as she repeats Megan's words. Because that's the winning ticket.

'But she didn't want them to read it,' I say.

'So why put it on the internet?'

'She didn't think they'd read it. They wouldn't have, except for you.'

'Don't you think the blog is good?' she asks.

'That's not the point!'

But Hazel goes on like it is the point. 'I think it's really good. And if she's embarrassed by it, that's not my fault.' She looks over my shoulder at Megan and puts on that fake concerned face again. 'Is she?'

'What?'

'Embarrassed?'

'Yes, by *you*!' I say.

But she's too fast for me. 'Really? Okay, I'll go back and apologize.' She starts off, and I do exactly what she wants me to do. I grab her arm.

'No, don't!' I say.

'Lucy!' She shakes her head like she's lost. 'What do you want me to do?'

How is she doing this? Twisting it back on me. She knows exactly what I mean, I can see it in the smile in her eyes.

'Just leave her alone,' I say.

She points to her house. 'That's what I was trying to do, Lucy. But if you think she needs me?' She raises her eyebrows.

'No, she's fine,' I say.

'Well, you better tell her to take it down if it upsets her that much,' she says.

Every part of me wants to say something that will snatch the smile from her face. But I don't. Because I don't have the right words.

Hazel walks out of the park. I'm shaking with anger. I don't feel bad about reading her diary any more, she deserves it. I have to get back to Megan. So I turn around. Then I realize she's already gone.

I run back to the guys. 'Where did Megan go?'

And I guess Guitar boy is not stupid because he says, 'The opposite direction to her.' He means Hazel. Megan must have left through the gate across from my house. So I run that way. But I don't see her on the street. I ring her phone, but she doesn't pick up. I send her a string of texts, but they all say the same thing and mean nothing. Because Hazel might not be worth getting upset over, but the horrible things she does and says are.

Slowly, I cross the road to my house. And I'm so angry at Hazel and worried for Megan, that I almost don't notice the book on Ms Cusack's doorstep.

Searching the windows for a face, I go up. Then I look left and right, just in case my dad has come home early again. But there's no one watching me.

I grab it and hop back down into the street again. Turning it over, I read the title. *Of Mice and Men*. And this time the note says, *I hope you are reading faster than I can eat.*

It's a small book but it feels heavy in my hand.

Behind the door, she's in there.

I move to my front door. Megan is missing. Mum's out. And I have one and a half books to get through now, so I might as well make a start.

120

CHAPTER 16

We've had dinner. One of those dinners where Dad doesn't tell Mum that he's going to pay back a loan to Mr Reynolds, and Mum doesn't tell Dad that she was gone most of the day all dressed up, and I don't tell anyone that we broke into Hazel's house.

The room is filled with silent *questionables* darting around between us.

Right now we are pretending to watch TV in the family room. It's *Who Wants to Be a Millionaire?* Mum's on one couch, Dad's on the other and I'm on a chair. Mum's holding her phone where Dad can't see it and she's checking it every few minutes, and Dad's got his laptop open beside him. I bet he's waiting for the money to arrive so he can send it to Mr Reynolds.

He looks over at Mum. He waits but she refuses to notice because she's still not talking to him. 'I'm getting ten million off Seanie,' he says.

It's hard to keep ignoring him now. Mum nods. 'Good,' she says and continues pretending to watch TV.

Maybe she doesn't care what that means. But I do. 'Does that mean you can flip The Old Mill, Dad?' And that soon, everything can go back to normal.

He lifts an eyebrow. 'Almost. Another few days.' He winks. Then he looks back at his screen and a smile cracks his face. 'Speak of the devil. There she is, the little beauty.'

He turns a grin on both of us. Mum doesn't even blink.

'Can I see?' I say and Dad's grin spreads. He pats the couch. I hop up and sit down beside him. His bank account is open. And it shows a transaction for ten million.

'So what now?' I ask.

Dad shoots a look at Mum. 'Eh, well, I'll use it for the next stage of development.'

But that's not what he said earlier to Oly. He said he'd transfer it immediately to Mr Reynolds.

'Do your old man a favour, go get us a coffee?' he says.

I can't really say *No*, so I go into the kitchen and by the time I come back with a tray and two coffees, Dad's sitting back with his arms spread over the back of the couch, wearing a lopsided grin. 'Ah, lovely stuff,' he says to me.

I sit beside him. He turns his laptop away from me.

'Any biscuits with that?' he asks. 'Actually, wait, I've just the thing.'

Dad slides his laptop onto the couch and leaves the room. Mum picks up her phone and starts texting. I hear Dad climb the stairs.

I want to see it. To know if Dad's lopsided smile is what *questionable* becoming *illegal* looks like. Above my head, I hear him move around.

Lifting his laptop, I click on the open web page to his bank account.

And there it is. He did it. Ten in. Ten out. The beginning of the end of The Old Mill.

I hear Dad move again. I picture his lopsided grin and I know that later tonight, I'll draw it and stick it up in the attic.

Then I have an idea.

In the bar at the top there's an option to 'Save as pdf'. I click it. Then I open my email account, attach the pdf and send it to myself. Dad's feet are on the stairs and my heart is in my mouth.

Deleting the pdf, I close my email account and slide the laptop onto the couch.

Later, when no one is around, I'll print it out and stick it beside my drawing.

Dad comes in holding one of those huge Toblerones he used to always bring me back from business trips. 'Saw it in the airport last time I went through,' he says and throws it onto my lap. 'Forgot to give it to you.'

My heart's still racing. 'Thanks, Dad.'

He shoves his laptop aside and makes a big deal of settling back down. He lets the contestant on the TV answer a question, then he nudges me. 'Give us a piece of your Toblerone.'

I break off three bits. 'Mum?'

She looks at me and smiles, but it's not a happy smile. I want so much to say, *Dad's fine, everything's going to be okay*. I want to show her the pdf.

But Mum shakes her head and looks back at the TV, and Dad elbows me and says, 'See if you can fit a whole piece in your mouth.'

He slides one side of a piece into his mouth, then another, until the corners make his cheeks stick out.

On TV, the presenter is asking the contestant, who is so nervous he keeps laughing, *Which country is the smallest country in Africa?*

Dad shouts an answer through his Toblerone.

'Which?' I say.

He holds up two fingers. He's picking Lesotho.

I shake my head, put a whole piece in my mouth and say, 'The Gambia,' but all that comes out is spit, so I hold up three fingers.

The guy on TV says, 'Fifty-fifty, please.' Ivory Coast and Senegal disappear.

'Lesotho,' Dad shouts again.

He's wrong. It's The Gambia. I learned it in school.

The nervous guy picks Lesotho. He loses fifteen thousand.

Dad shakes his head and I look at the laptop on the couch. I definitely deleted the pdf, didn't I? But I did, I know I did . . .

Dad eats the whole piece of chocolate in one go like we used to do when I was a kid. He's halfway through his coffee by the time I finally swallow the last of mine.

'Too slow,' he says. He leans back and rubs his belly. 'Stuffed.' And that lopsided smile is back on his face. The smile that matches *ten in, ten out*.

Then it's quiet. No one says anything. Not even the guy on the TV. Because he's thinking he doesn't know the answer, and Dad's thinking about The Old Mill, and Mum's texting someone, and I'm thinking, *So that's what questionable becoming illegal looks like*, so loud, I'm sure Dad'll hear.

'Think I'll go read,' I say.

WEDNESDAY

CHAPTER 17

The house is quiet when I wake up. I grab some juice and go to the conservatory to draw.

Last night I drew a picture of Dad's lopsided grin. I had him sitting on a beach in Brazil, holding a cocktail, with the sea twinkling behind him.

Now I draw Hazel's face, the moment she realized that Megan was making fun of her and she decided to read Megan's blog to the boys. She knew what she was doing. And she enjoyed it.

But the more I draw, the more I see Megan's grin when she was making fun of Hazel for liking Stephen. Which she only knew because she read her diary. We read her diary.

The thing is, I know Hazel deserves it in a way. But I don't think it makes it right. Megan mocking Hazel was kind of like what Hazel is doing to Megan. And I laughed. I joined in.

On the other hand, Megan said she wanted to be sure of the truth. Now she's sure. So she can stand up to Hazel, which is good. Or, seeing as Hazel will deny it, maybe Megan can just stop hanging around with her now. Which is fine by me. Although we might not have a choice because school starts soon. I groan at the idea of being stuck in a class with Hazel for the next six years. Hopefully we'll take different subjects. She'd definitely take Music. I want to choose Art, though I know what Dad will say. But maybe if I told him that I want to get the highest marks in my exams so that I can get into a good course in university, and Art would be a sure bet, he'd let me. It'd help if I won the Young Artist of the Year this year.

'Penny for your thoughts?' Mum's at the door.

I've about a million thoughts. I choose one. 'I'm wondering if I could come first in the Young Artist of the Year Award this year.'

'You've a better chance than most. When do they announce the theme?'

'Soon,' I say. 'Actually, they might have done it already.'

'Well, find out when they announce it. And if they haven't announced it yet, draw one picture a day until they do.'

'Deal.'

'You can start today,' she says, like me having a plan has cheered her up.

'What are you doing today?'

Mum looks up at the ceiling and blows out air. 'Your father's accounts,' she says like she's saying, *Getting a tooth out.* Mum's been doing his accounts since he set up his

130

own company. She wanted to go back to work and he said, *This way, you have a job and can still be at home with Lucy. It's win-win.*

I wonder are they talking to each other yet. Mum's still staring at the ceiling with that going-to-the-dentist look. I don't know if she's worried about the accounts or Dad's mood or both. 'Everything will be okay now that he's paid Mr Reynolds his ten million, Mum. He said it'll only be a few days until he flips The Old Mill.'

Her eyes drop. Her head turns. She blinks.

I blink.

What did I just say? I wasn't supposed to mention Mr Reynolds. Or the loan.

'I mean, he'll be less stressed now that he has the money from Sean, and when he flips The Old Mill, everything will be back to normal.'

She's staring at me.

I concentrate on drawing until she goes back into the kitchen.

It's almost lunchtime when Megan texts, which is the first I've heard from her since she ran out of the park yesterday.

Megan
New blog up!

She must be feeling better about Hazel if she's written a blog!

Closing over my sketch pad, I go into the family room, turn on the computer and bring up her blog.

It's called *Penny Joins the Orchestra*, and the more I read, the more the baby snakes inside me squirm and divide and multiply. Because she has used the information from Hazel's diary.

In the blog, Penny falls in love with the First Chair violinist, but she accidently exposes the label on her super-padded bra to everyone and they all laugh at her.

It's funny. But she's doing it again. Using Hazel's secrets to make fun of her in the same way Hazel bullies Megan, by pretending she's not doing anything.

Back in the conservatory, I call her.

'Well?' she says after two rings. 'You like it?'

She sounds happy. She sounds like her old self. And I almost don't say what I'm thinking. Almost. 'We shouldn't have done it.'

'Done what?'

'Read her diary.'

'Yes,' she says. 'We should.'

'Well, you shouldn't have written about it,' I say.

There's a pause, then, 'Wait, what did you say to Hazel in the park yesterday?' she says, as if I sided with Hazel or something.

'I told her that she embarrassed you on purpose and to stop,' I say.

'Right, so what's the problem?'

I watch a cat on the wall in the back garden, and I try to figure out what I want to say. 'I understand how annoyed you are. Hazel's horrible. But we were only supposed to find

132

out for sure that it's her trolling you. You weren't supposed to use her private information on your blog.'

'I didn't. It's fiction, inspired by reality. Like all my blogs.'

'Megan, it's different.'

Megan goes quiet for so long that I'm about to say, *hello*, when she speaks.

'How about this, fact or fiction?' she says. '*Oh, God, poor Penny. You know they are laughing at you, not with you, right?*'

'Okay, I know, but—'

'Or, this, *Why doesn't a friend tell you to stop trying so hard? Oh, yeah, duh, you'd need to actually have a friend first.*'

I stay quiet because Megan's getting upset. And she has a point.

'I mean, is that anonymous or personal?' Megan says.

I watch the cat scale the wall and don't reply.

'It was also *you* that said I should do something,' she says.

'Yeah,' I finally say. 'I know, it's just . . . I don't think it's the right way.'

'So what should I do?'

'Say something to her.'

'She'll deny it. At least this way, if she puts up any more comments now, she's really slagging herself. It might actually stop her.'

Oh, I don't know. Maybe she's right. And maybe, once school starts, Hazel will just hang out with her orchestra friends and it'll all be fine.

I look at Hazel's face on the sketch pad. I remember how

133

she twisted my words. Flicking the page over, my drawing from last night looks back at me. Dad's lopsided grin.

On the other end of the line, Megan says, 'What are you doing?'

'Nothing, just thinking.'

'I mean, today,' she says.

But I don't want to see her. Not right now. I'm too confused.

'I'm going to the gallery to see if they've any information on this year's competition. I'll call you later.' I hang up before she can speak. I need to get some air. Shouting to Mum that I'm going to the gallery, I head outside and I'm passing Ms Cusack's when I notice something.

Her door's open.

Stepping closer, I can almost smell the cat pee, taste the mould.

Why is the door open? Did she leave it open for me? Is she inviting me to come in? I look around but there's no one at the windows watching me.

She must be in there. I don't think I want to meet her. Well, I kind of do but I kind of don't. I mean, what if I go in there and she starts shrieking at me like she did to Dad? I step away from the door. But then I think of her notes. *I hope you are reading as fast as I'm eating.* She doesn't sound crazy. Not completely crazy, anyway. And I think of the homeless man's message in chalk. *Spare a kind word.*

I sigh. Why can't I figure out what the right thing to do is? Maybe talking to her is the right thing.

And, to be honest, part of me wants to see for myself: the

house, the artist, what it means to make the wro

I could just say, *hi*. Thank her for the books. Ask
she needs anything from the shops . . . Taking a deep breath,
I knock on the door.

It swings wide.

And I can't believe what I see.

CHAPTER 18

The furniture stands like art. Embroidered couches, golden curtains, lamps like velvet magicians' hats.

There are newspapers. Yellowed. But they are framed and take up almost a whole wall.

And in the centre of it all is a grand staircase that rises and splits as it swoops left and right up to the first floor. A thick red carpet lines it.

It's completely different to ours. No halls, no rooms, no doors. Just areas to sit or to read or to paint.

I can't hear anything, except ... openness. The house feels open, not shut away. I should turn. Go. But I can't. I need to see. Because this is the last thing I ever expected.

Stepping gingerly onto the stairs, I reach out for the banisters. Solid mahogany.

I shouldn't do this. But still I go up, step by step, as silently as I can, until I reach the top. Right now, more than anything in the world, I want to see her. Because this doesn't look like the house of a penniless waster.

Upstairs, it's a library. With more books than I've ever seen in my life. The walls are covered from floor to ceiling. There's a sliding ladder, and wood and leather everywhere. Reading nooks are carved out of towers of novels. A deep couch to sit on and look at millions of words all bound up and waiting to be freed, like birds in a sanctuary.

This is a place that stores words. That loves them.

In the corners are spiral staircases that lead to the next floor. But I don't dare go any further. Instead, I pad back down the stairs.

Where is she?

I should call out, say I'm here. No, I shouldn't, I should leave.

The air is warm and lazy as if it carries old conversations. I move around the stairs into the main room. *There are these masks on the walls . . . ancient newspapers everywhere . . . the top floors are rotten . . .* I reach out and touch the base of the staircase, solid as a tree. Hanging on it, watching me from a framed canvas, is a man smoking a pipe with a face lined like streams running into a river.

Not masks. Portraits. And Dad's wrong, the eyes don't follow me, they see right through me. And all the lies I believed.

In one of the framed newspapers there's a photograph of a woman. Her fist is raised and clenched. She's protesting. I recognize her. She's the woman from the painting in the attic.

And beneath the framed newspaper is a table with an unopened bottle of tawny port.

'Lonely,' I whisper. I shake my head as the word spins through the room before fading. 'Witch. Spinster. Penniless. Crazy.' Each word dissolves like a cold breath on a warm day. They lied. All of them. Dad and Oly and Mr Reynolds. They lied about a woman who lives alone and paints by herself and has never done anything to them.

But that's a lie too, right? Because I think of Dad, drinking his beer and saying, *I'd give her one point five million in the morning*, and suddenly I know what happened. He came in here and tried to buy her house and she told him where to go. And when Oly called her *wild*, what he really meant was he couldn't believe she'd value her home more than Dad's money.

Something moves in the garden. I make no sound as I cross to the window.

I freeze.

It's her.

It's really her.

She's standing with her back to me. Her long skirt flows in the wind but is pinched tight at the waist. Her hair is gathered in a huge bun on her head and long earrings almost touch her shoulders. She's as still as a statue. She's painting.

By her feet, the cat I saw on the wall earlier slinks along, his raised tail brushing off her skirt. She's painting what she sees: her garden, bursting with leaves and flowers and bushes and birds. Her tall figure blocks my view of something so I step to the side.

There's a tunnel. Through the bushes. It leads straight down to the back gate.

That's how she comes and goes. It is so obvious, I'm stunned. I've probably even seen her before, outside. I just wasn't looking for a tall, elegant woman.

She doesn't use her front door. Which means she must have left it open for someone. Maybe it was for me. Maybe she wants to meet me.

Bending down now, she pets her cat. My heart races at the thought of her turning. Seeing me. Seeing through me.

Because I felt sorry for her. For being lonely and crazy. For making mistakes. For being an artist, a penniless painter.

Quietly, I turn, and the eyes of the portraits follow me as I go back to the door carrying the truth inside me.

I close it gently so she'll never know I came into her home. Because maybe she did leave it open for me. But I don't belong here.

CHAPTER 19

I'm like a pumpkin, carved up and empty, as I come away from Ms Cusack's. All their lies. And I believed them.

How easily Dad told them. *There I was, shaking like a kid in a witch's house,* like the truth had no right to get in his way.

And it's not even the lies. It's the way he spat them out. *Waster.* The way he laughed at her. Because she's an artist.

Our front door is open. I didn't leave it open. I walk over. And as I step up, I see Dad's briefcase is thrown on the floor by the door and a layer of words, like smoke, hits me in the face.

'Declan, you can't do this!' Mum's shouting.

'I'm *this* close to flipping The Old Mill, Alice. We're talking *days.* And then I can bid on another that's three times as big. So just calm down, okay?'

They are in the living room. I step into the front hall next to the table.

'Calm down?' Mum says.

'I'm handling it. Back off,' Dad says.

'And it's not just the astonishing amount. It's what you've done with it. Do you understand that?' Mum says.

'Oh, please, don't start telling me how to—'

'Misappropriating funds left, right and centre?' Mum says. 'What the hell are you thinking?'

I can hear Mum shaking from here. The walls vibrate with it.

Dad's tone switches to the one that makes people back away slowly. 'What the hell were *you* doing, snooping?'

'Snooping? It's my job,' Mum says. 'And don't you dare do that!'

'Do what, exactly?' Dad says.

'Change the subject,' she says.

Through the gap, I see them. She's beside the mantelpiece with her back against the wall. He's in front of her so I can't see his face. But hers is wide open.

'You've gone too far, Declan,' she says and he's so close, he must feel her words on his face. 'I won't let you—'

'Let me?' His words pop like knuckles cracking. '*Let* me?' His fist is clenched.

All the blood in my body drops to my feet. I steady myself on the hall table, making the vase on top of it wobble.

Mum tries to move back.

'*Declan*—' Mum doesn't speak it, she breathes it.

'Is that what you said? Say it again. Go on.'

She doesn't speak. She doesn't move.

His clenched hand is rising.

I do the only thing I can think of doing. I slap the vase to the floor.

It topples. It falls. Then *CRASH!* A thousand splinters fly through the hall.

There's a second where the world freezes. Then Dad comes storming past me, and I see his face, all sliced up by lines of anger as deep as scars. He slams the front door behind him.

Mum doesn't speak. She pushes herself off the wall and walks dead straight, then lowers herself onto a chair. Her breathing is broken, it comes in bursts.

I move up beside her.

'I knocked a vase over.'

She nods.

'He's gone out,' I say.

I wait for her to say something. But she doesn't speak at all. Just sits in simmering silence. The clock ticks and the traffic beeps and the silence bubbles over with all the words she doesn't say.

She reaches out to me and pulls me down, hugs me and kisses my head. Then she holds me at arm's length and she smiles. But it's not really a smile. It's just a bad lie.

Then she goes upstairs. I stay standing above the empty chair.

He's gone out. But it's not over, is it? We've just pressed pause. Because he has another one. A bigger development.

I feel like I'm in a theatre after the actors and audience

have left. The lines have been delivered. You can still smell the last scene. But it's quiet. It's all make-believe. Until tomorrow.

Taking out my phone, I call Megan. I don't even let her speak, as soon as she picks up, I say, 'I need you. Meet me in the park in fifteen minutes.'

CHAPTER 20

I'm pacing beneath the trees in the park but it doesn't matter how fast I walk, the words stay with me.

He would have hit her.

I thought it would get better but it won't. Because now he has another development, three times as big.

I go out of the park to wait for Megan. Standing on the path, I look at Ms Cusack's house. The red brick is stained to ash and the paint around the windows is peeling. Hers is the bad tooth, but it smells of varnish that's seeped into wood and canvas over years and years. Ours tastes of the bleach that can't lift all the lies that have been told. Lies that I'm a part of.

He would have hit her.

Megan pedals around the corner. As she locks her bike to a lamp post, I cross the road.

'What's wrong?' she asks as she turns.

Where do I start? I don't know, so instead of talking, I walk.

Had I really thought it would get better? That it was just the stress? It doesn't even matter that he has a new, bigger deal coming, though. Because his studded words and clenched fist were not because of stress. They were because Mum questioned him. Stood up to him. He was going to hit her because she told him that what he is doing is wrong.

And I didn't stop him. I just smashed a vase. It'll happen again.

'Lucy?' Megan says.

We're halfway down the street behind our house and I still don't know what to tell her. So I start somewhere else. 'I went into Ms Cusack's house.'

Stopping, I turn to her.

'Okay,' she says like she's pretty sure that I'm not telling her the real problem.

'It's beautiful, Megan. Full of art. Paintings, furniture, books. I saw her there, painting. She looked –' what's the opposite to a waster? – 'real,' I say.

Megan frowns. 'I thought you said she was poor?'

'I did. She's not.'

Megan speaks slowly because she's not sure where this is going. Or what it's got to do with me being upset. 'So why did you think she was?'

I study the roofs of the Georgian buildings across the road. 'He called her a waster. He said all these things about her that weren't true. Because she's an artist.'

'Who?'

I look back at Megan. 'Dad.'

'Oh,' Megan says. Then she says 'Oh,' again like she finally gets what I mean. 'Lucy, it doesn't matter what he thinks.'

But she doesn't get it. 'Yes, it does, it's all that matters. What he thinks. What mood he's in.'

'I know, but—'

'Megan,' I say in a voice so small it's almost lost. 'He was going to hit her.' I'm biting my lip now. I can't look at her, so I walk fast again. 'He was going to hit her. Then I smashed a vase.'

'Lucy! That's . . . are you okay?' she says, running to catch up. 'I mean, what happened?'

'They were fighting about money, and . . .' But it wasn't about money, was it? It was about what he did. *Misappropriating funds.* I'm not supposed to know. And I'm definitely not supposed to tell. But I'm sick of keeping Dad's lie. So, finally, I tell her the truth: all about the cellar and Mr Reynolds. And then I tell her about Dad paying off the loan and me printing out the pdf. 'Mum didn't know until today,' I say. 'I kind of told her by accident, and she does his books, so she figured the rest of it out. Or maybe it was something else that he'd done that she found out about, I'm not sure. Whatever it was, she was asking him about it and they were shouting and he went to hit her but I came in.'

Megan stops walking, and after a few steps, I do too. I turn to her.

'Is she okay?' she asks.

'Yeah,' I say. 'This time.' And we both hear the words I can't say. *What about next time?*

'When did it happen?'

'Just now. I walked in on them and Dad stormed out.'

'That's . . .' she says, and searches for the word.

Awful, frightening, wrong. All of them at once. Whatever that word is.

'I know,' I say.

We start walking again but slower this time. Neither of us speaks until we turn onto the street that leads back to mine. Then Megan says, 'Have you talked to your mum about it?'

'No,' I say. 'Never. It's like we've silently promised that if we don't talk about it, it's not real.'

Megan shakes her head like she can't believe we could ignore it. But ignoring is easy compared to actually sitting down with Mum and saying the words, *He would have hit you.* And I've no idea why it's like that. But it is. 'Maybe it's because it was easier to ignore when it wasn't so bad. And now that it's bad, it's like it's too hard to stop ignoring.'

We get to the corner and stop.

'Do you think she'll do something about your dad breaking the law?'

'Like what?'

'Tell someone? The police, maybe?'

I almost laugh. 'No way. Anyway, I don't think what he's doing is really bad. I think it's like cheating at Monopoly.'

Megan gives me a look because she doesn't understand.

'You know, like a speeding ticket. It's breaking the law, but it's not that bad.'

Megan nods to say she gets it.

'He said something about hanging out in Brazil for a year if he got caught.'

Megan thinks about this for a bit and then nods again.

'I'd say that he'd probably worry more about people knowing he did something wrong than about getting in trouble with the law,' I say.

Back at the park, it's almost empty. We go through the gate and sit. I pull out a clump of grass and let it slide through my fingers. The breeze carries it a little before it reaches the ground.

'What are you going to do?' Megan asks, but I don't have an answer and suddenly I'm biting my lip again and looking away. Then I feel Megan's hand on mine. 'Maybe he'll get caught anyway. And end up in prison.' But she's joking. Or at least half-joking.

I blink a few times and then turn back to her. 'Get taken from our house in handcuffs?'

'You'd be on the six o'clock news, smiling in the background,' she says.

'I'd have to smuggle things into prison that he needs. Like his Domaine de la Romanée and the special coffee that he has flown in from Africa.'

'And moisturized toilet paper. Prison paper is awful,' Megan says.

'I bet prison clothes aren't even real cotton. *Poxy polyester*,' I say.

'And the colour?' Megan says. 'Just awful.'

I smile. But not for long. 'He's too clever to get caught.' I let another handful of grass fall through my fingers.

Where did he go when he stormed out, to the Local? Will he stay out for the evening or is he back already? 'It's going to get worse,' I say. Then I take a deep breath. 'And how do I stop him next time? Smash another vase? Shout at him? Say I'll tell the world that he's a criminal?'

Megan tilts her head like she's considering that.

'I'm joking,' I say. 'That's like me pointing a gun at him when he knows that I won't pull the trigger.'

'I know, but still.'

'Still, what?'

'It would be nice to have a gun, right? Like having insurance,' she says.

I imagine standing in front of him, holding up the printout of his bank statement. And him taking it from me with a grin on his face. He wouldn't raise his fist. He'd lift his foot and crush me like an ant.

'Besides,' I say, 'I only have a printout showing money coming into his account and going out. But you can't tell where it goes. I'd need a copy of Mr Reynolds's statement to match up the account numbers and prove it went to him.'

Megan chews this over for a while, then she says, 'Who is Mr Reynolds anyway?'

'A property developer, like Dad, I think. Except Mr

Reynolds is bigger. And he practically owns a bank.' Then I look across at our row. 'And he lives there.'

She looks where I'm pointing. 'In that house at the end?'

'Yeah.'

'Huh.'

We both watch the house for a while.

I wonder did Dad owe Mr Reynolds or his bank? I think it was Mr Reynolds, though. I'd know for sure if I saw his bank statement. A ten million deposit to match Dad's payment of ten million. But that's not going to happen. I mean, how would I get into his account like I did to Dad's? I couldn't.

After a minute, though, I remember that Mum gets her statements through the post, because recently she said that she *must go green and switch to online statements*.

I lean sideways so I can see around a bush. There's his front door. And there's his letterbox. 'Mr Reynolds is pretty old,' I say. Megan doesn't respond, so I explain. 'So he might prefer the old-fashioned way of getting statements.'

'Which is?'

'Which is through the letterbox.'

After a few seconds, she gets what I mean. She leans sideways so she can see the letterbox too.

'So if I wanted proof . . .' I say.

She looks at me. 'Not that you would use it or anything . . .'

'No,' I say.

She turns back to his house. 'But if you wanted it . . .'

'Yeah. If I did. That's where it would be.' We both watch

the front door for a while. It's just a little after four p.m. so not many people are passing by.

'And it would be sitting on the floor of his hallway until he got home from work,' Megan says.

'Which is probably around five p.m.'

'It would just sit there all day,' Megan says.

'Waiting to be picked up,' I say.

'By Mr Reynolds,' she says.

'Or someone else.'

A woman passes his front door. I lose sight of her behind a bush. Then the street is quiet.

At the same time, me and Megan look at each other. And I know we're thinking the same thing. That even if I got my hands on that statement, I'd probably never do anything with it. Because I'd never actually fire a bullet.

But, still. It would be nice to have a gun.

CHAPTER 21

I'm following the beam of my torch through the darkness, all the way down to the opposite end of the attics. To Mr Reynolds's. I stop above his ceiling panel.

Maybe he has motion sensors in his house. I'll get arrested. And then what will I say?

I take out my phone and call Megan, who is outside watching his front door. She picks up immediately. 'Are you there?'

'I'm in his attic.'

'Haven't seen him,' she says. 'But that doesn't mean he's not in there. What if he came back early?'

My hand is on the panel. But she's right. 'Go ring his doorbell,' I say. 'If he answers just say *wrong house* and then call me.' I hang up and wait. And as I do, I picture me in his hallway with his alarm going off and the police arriving and them calling my dad and him exploding with anger . . .

Megan calls back. 'No one answered the door.'

'Okay,' I say. 'Okay,' I repeat. 'I'm going in.'

Hanging up, I force myself to open the ceiling panel and, before I can change my mind, drop through into the room below.

It's a small library and it smells like it was last used in 1950. But there's a chair I can use to climb out on. That's good. That's something.

Just a quick look, then I'll leave. Out in the hall, I go straight for the stairs.

Wait, what if his statement arrived before today? It might already be in a drawer somewhere, which means I need to check the whole house. Quickly.

There are paintings on the walls as I go down the stairs. Old ones. Of people. Not beautiful, like the lined faces in Ms Cusack's. Probably his ancestors, watching me as I steal down the stairs.

By the time I get to the second floor, my heart's already hammering. A door creaks as I push it open. It's a private cinema. I won't find anything in here. On the other side is a gym and stretch of grass. My brain is spinning and it takes me a second to realize that it's for practising golf.

I go downstairs. Two guest bedrooms. The master bedroom. I go in. Slippers lined up below the bed. Pyjamas laid out on the fresh sheets. And on the wall, a framed cheque for one million euro.

At the window, I risk a peek. Megan is there, watching the street below me. I'm okay.

I glance around the room and open a few drawers. No letters or statements.

Leaving the thick carpet of the bedroom, I tiptoe down the polished wood stairs into the front hall. The post is sitting there on the hall floor. I grab it and flick through. Nothing says anything about a bank on it. Standing this close to the front door, my breath comes faster. I look towards the kitchen.

I shouldn't go in there. Even if Megan rings me the second that he comes around the corner or steps out of a car, I'll barely have enough time to get out before he's at the front door.

But he's old and I'm fast. One quick look, then I'm gone.

My chest stings and my heart is pounding so hard as I move through the hallway that it's difficult to breathe. I pass the cellar door. I stop.

Mr Reynolds has a wine cellar. Maybe he has an office down there too. I had better check. Opening the door gently, I tiptoe down.

This is nothing like Dad's wine cellar. Dad's is made of wood but this one's like a vault or something. There are three arches, with alcoves off each. I creep past the first two. The wine racks are built into the stone with these tiny lights sunk into the walls. In each alcove there are little tables with two empty wine glasses on each. At the other end there's a big dining table with a table cloth and it's laid out with empty plates and glasses.

And behind it, built into the wall, is a safe with one

of those twisty combination locks. That's where I'd keep documents if I was him. I have no idea how to break into one, though. I look around again but there are no drawers anywhere.

As I turn, though, I see a decanter on the shelf in the corner filled with wine.

Which means the wine is breathing.

Which means someone intends on drinking it soon.

I look at the table. There's a plate on it with some cheese and grapes.

Oh, no.

I whip out my phone. There's no signal. I sprint to the other end of the room until I see a bar appear. I run up the steps. A text from Megan arrives at the exact same moment that I hear voices in the hall.

Megan
Get out, he's coming! He's with two other men!

I fly back down the steps. Above me, the door opens.

No, no, no!

I run through the room.

There are voices. Footsteps on the stairs. I only have time to jump behind the last pillar when they start walking through the vault.

I'm trapped!

Over the pounding of my heart, I hear their footsteps. Then they stop. They're chatting. I search around me. My

155

eyes fall on the tablecloth. It reaches almost to the ground. It's my only option.

Taking a deep breath, I peek around the pillar. Mr Reynolds is in the middle of the vault. He has his back to me and he's holding a briefcase. I can't see the others, they must be behind a pillar. Now or never.

I drop to the ground and crawl as fast as I can between two chairs and under the table. I scoot to the other side so that I've a better chance of being hidden.

They're coming. They get closer. Three sets of shoes stop by the table. Something is dropped on it and the table shakes.

'How many times does it work for them?' one voice says.

'One in twenty?' the other says.

'So why keep kicking it? Nineteen times out of twenty, they lose possession. Look at the France game, if we had just held on ...'

I've been around my dad's friends enough to know they're talking about rugby. I watch one set of shoes go to the side of the room and there's a gurgle as wine is poured.

'Cheers, Charlie,' one of the men says. That's Mr Reynolds's first name, I think. 'Ooh, that's a good glass of wine. By the way, the new house red at the Local? Absolute muck.'

I squeeze myself until I'm as small as possible.

They're talking about rugby again. I take a peek. They wander around as they discuss tactics.

Then Mr Reynolds's voice cuts across them. 'Anyway, this is just a quick chat to consolidate a few matters.' It's the voice he uses in cellars. 'I understand there have been some ... *concerns* ... raised by you both, regarding the money I owe to BBR.'

I hold my breath and listen. And it's the gravel in his voice that makes me slip out my phone and open the microphone setting. I hold my finger against *record*. The red light on the screen flashes.

'Our only *concern*, Charlie, is that you owe over eighty million at this stage and that this might raise a few eyebrows.'

'You're right,' Mr Reynolds says, and I hear what I think is the clasps on his briefcase clicking open. 'Which is why I've secured a temporary loan from our friends over at HMB. Eighty million has been lodged into BBR today and will remain there until after the audit on the thirtieth. So, along with the ten million that I received from Fitzsimmons yesterday ...'

He just said that he got money off Dad! I double-check that the light on my phone is still red. It is.

Mr Reynolds goes on, talking about Dad going bankrupt and BBR taking The Old Mill off his hands. Someone blows out air like he's impressed.

'Reynolds, you're a legend,' one man says.

There are a few sighs and a few chuckles, then a clinking of glasses. 'Cheers,' they say together.

'Now, gentlemen, I trust that settles all concerns?'

'And then some,' someone says.

'Well, then, if you'd like to make your way upstairs, I will be with you in a moment.'

157

The other men take a few seconds to finish up. Then they move away from the table and walk through the vault. Once they start climbing the stairs, Mr Reynolds walks around to this side of the table. He stops right beside me. He opens his safe, drops something into it, slams it shut and then leaves.

I watch him go through the vault. He climbs the stairs. Closes the door.

I wait.

Time passes and I hear nothing from upstairs. I crawl out and sprint back through the room until I have reception. A text comes through from a few minutes ago.

Megan
Are you okay?!!
They just went into the Local.

My heart is racing and my hands are shaking, but I'm okay.

What's more, I think I have a gun.

Me and Megan are back in my attic huddled on the beanbag and we've just listened to the voice recording on my phone for the third time.

'He definitely says the words, *along with the ten million that I received from Fitzsimmons yesterday*,' Megan says. 'You have it.'

I have proof Dad did something illegal.

'So, what now?' she says.

We both look at the phone sitting on the floor.

'No idea,' I say.

A gun would probably be more useful to me than this. I mean, it's proof that my dad did something illegal, right? So that means that my dad's a criminal now?

But he can't be. And if he was, I wouldn't actually want him to get caught, would I?

I picture his clenched fist. What would he do if he knew I even had this, let alone if I threatened him with it?

Still, knowing I have something if I ever do need to use it makes me feel a little better.

There's a knock on my bedroom door below. Megan and I scramble out as quickly and quietly as we can and when I've closed the ceiling panel, I open the door.

It's Mum. She looks wrecked. But not as limp as earlier.

She smiles, and I see a flicker of brightness in her eyes as if she's going to tell me something. But then she notices Megan behind me.

'Megan! I didn't know you were here,' she says. And when she looks back at me the flicker is gone. 'Fancy a pizza?'

She turns and whatever she was going to say leaves with her.

THURSDAY

CHAPTER 22

Megan slept over last night. Now she's nudging me. I groan and roll over. She nudges me again. When I open my eyes, there's a phone in front in my face.

It's only 8.32.

'Read it,' she says. 'It's another comment.'

I sigh and sit up.

How about a new blog called The Penny Behind the Pen, *where Penny is this loser with no life who writes blogs that no one reads.*

I hand it back, but Megan says, 'There are others. Below it.'

I scroll down and read a few more. *The next blog could be about Penny starting school, hoping to find friends, but when she gets there she realizes they've all read her pathetic blog and no one will sit beside her!* It goes on like that, so many comments that Hazel must have been awake half the night.

Megan takes her phone back and stares at the screen. 'So

it didn't work, writing that blog about her. She's not going to stop, is she?'

'I don't know, Megan.' I can't think about Hazel right now. Because it's after eight a.m. Dad must be up. That's assuming he came home. He hadn't by the time we went to bed. 'I'm going downstairs to see what's going on.'

At the kitchen door, I see Dad. He's got his back to us. The radio is on. He's staring into the distance and shaking his head. 'Jesus,' he whispers and takes a gulp of coffee. Then he raises it towards the radio and nods.

The man on the radio is talking about a housing bubble.

Is Mum okay? Did they have another fight when he got back last night? I go in, startling Dad, and he almost spills his coffee.

'Morning, girls,' he says.

Dad's hand on his coffee mug is so big, it nearly wraps all the way around. I used to love his hands. How strong they were. When I was small, I thought they could fix anything.

'Stealman Brothers bank is collapsing,' Dad says. He gulps back his coffee then walks into the hall and upstairs.

Megan lifts her eyebrows but doesn't risk saying anything. We just get bowls and cereal and start eating.

The headline on the paper on the counter top says, STEALMAN ON VERGE OF COLLAPSE. The column at the side says, ARE MORE BANKS AT RISK?

Mum comes downstairs.

'You're up early, sleep well?' she says. She's dressed and I can't tell from her face if they are still fighting or ignoring each other or pretending that he didn't nearly hit her yesterday.

'Yeah,' I lie.

Dad's coming back. As he enters the kitchen, Mum bites her bottom lip and buries her head in her handbag.

'Not good at all,' Dad says as if we are part of the conversation in his head. 'If Stealmans collapses, it'll be a domino effect. Then who'll be investing?'

Mum doesn't answer. And by the way they ignore each other, I know they didn't fight again. Because they are too busy pretending nothing happened.

Dad grabs his keys. 'Stupid timing,' he says and leaves through the back. A few seconds later, Mum makes an excuse and leaves through the front.

When she's gone, Megan says, 'Your parents. They're like magnets. If they're not stuck together fighting, they've got their backs to each other.'

My spoon hovers around my chin as I stare at her.

'What?' she asks.

'That was really good,' I say. 'That's exactly what they're like.'

'Don't sound so surprised,' Megan says through a gob full of cereal. Then she lowers her voice. 'You okay?'

I shrug. I feel like I'm standing on top of a wall waiting to see which way I'll fall.

The kitchen is quiet while we eat.

'Well,' she says as she puts her bowl in the dishwasher,

'I have been dying to know if Lisette has found out about Hazel's crush on Stephen yet.'

It takes me a second to figure out what she means. 'Megan, we are not breaking into Hazel's house again.'

She raises her eyebrows until they almost meet her hair line. 'Why? You broke into Mr Reynolds's.'

'I know, but . . .'

'But what?'

'I didn't go through his private things.'

She laughs. 'Lucy! You went through his whole house! You recorded his words! That's much worse!'

'But it's not . . .' I stop. Because I realize she's right.

Megan looks at the clock. 'It's after nine.' She takes out her phone and rings someone. After a while, she says, 'No one is answering at Hazel's house. They are all out.' And then she stands and gives me a look that means, *Let's go.*

I don't move.

'Come on, you read those comments this morning,' she says. 'And, anyway, I helped you.'

I shake my head. This is wrong. I know it's wrong. But Megan's already out of the kitchen and up the stairs. I listen to her cross the first-floor landing. Then, sighing, I follow.

When we get to Hazel's attic, I try to talk her out of it again but she ignores me and drops into Hazel's house. So I jump down too and place the chair beneath the ceiling panel while Megan goes downstairs. By the time I catch up with her, she's on the second-floor landing. I'm about to speak when I hear something. A creak. Like someone rolling over in bed. Megan tiptoes to Hazel's room and I go to Stefanie's and stick my head around the door.

She's in bed!

Holding my breath, I creep out and move as fast as I can over to Hazel's room. 'Stefanie!' I mouth and point to her room. Megan just nods, opens the drawer and takes Hazel's diary out. Didn't she understand? 'Megan!' But I say it too quietly for her to hear.

She places the diary on the bed and finds the last page. Then she holds up her phone, takes a photo. Quickly and quietly, she replaces the diary. Then she looks at me. 'Okay!' she mouths and gives me the thumbs up.

And we're creeping back upstairs and climbing into the attic and Stefanie never wakes. It's too easy, this breaking and entering and stealing. We're going to get caught.

'We are not doing this again,' I say. 'Either of us.'

But Megan's giggling in the darkness so I grab her hand and drag her back to my attic. As soon as we get there, Megan sits on the beanbag and drops her phone onto her lap and starts reading.

Lisette and Stephen got back together!!!

I'm so upset. I can hardly write. I can't stop crying.

After everything he said to me! He told me I wasn't like other girls. That I was more mature. That he could talk to me easier than he could talk to his best friends!

We were supposed to meet to go to the violin shop again but he never turned up. I waited until it closed. I texted him three times but he didn't reply.

Then I got a text from Lisette that said she'd just got back with Stephen!

This morning I went in early to orchestra practice so I could find out what was going on, but neither of them were there. Then they turned up late with these big smiles on their faces and everyone knew straight away that they were a couple again. A few of Lisette's friends actually ran up and hugged her.

Lisette came up to me at the break. She said Stephen told her that being apart showed him that he was ready to commit. Then she said he told her that he could talk to her easier than he could his best friends!

She also said Stephen is having a party after the show for the second years, which means I'm not invited.

I started crying and Lisette got really embarrassed. I knew that she was worried what the others would think because she brought me to the bathroom. She said she was sorry I wasn't invited but that it was no big deal because once we were in school we'd have different friends anyway. She said that's the way it is and that I'll understand when school starts.

Then she said that we could still hang out on the weekends!

Break ended and Lisette gave me one of her looks to say I should grow up, and she went back inside.

And at the end, Stephen saw me but ignored me and they left together holding hands.

Megan is grinning up at me. 'I could not have made that up. It's almost the perfect next blog for Penny.'

'Megan!' I say.

'What?' she says, still smiling.

Why doesn't she get that it's private? 'You can't post that.'

The light from the lamp glints in her eyes, like a spark in a fire. 'Yes, I can.'

Shaking my head, I look through the darkness of the attics. Each has a panel. A lid keeping secrets locked inside. Until we opened them.

'Come on, Lucy. You've seen what she's writing about me. How is this any worse?'

I breathe deep. But the air in the attic doesn't feel free any more. I'm suffocating. 'It's not any worse, Megan,' I say. 'It's the same.' I shake my head as I look down at her. 'Which makes you as bad as her.'

Megan's grin is gone. She looks where I was looking, along the length of the attics, and chews her cheek for a minute. 'Fine,' she finally says, spreading her arms wide. 'Tell me what I'm supposed to do.'

'Stand up to her, face to face,' I say. But I don't even know what those words mean now.

'Like you did with your dad?' she throws back.

I open my mouth to reply. Then the impact of her words hits

me in the stomach. I turn. Dad's smug face looks down on me from the rafters, daring me to do something.

'Lucy?' Megan says.

I don't reply. I just shrink smaller and smaller, while Dad's face grows until it fills the whole attic, and the words, *Go on, I dare you*, get so loud and so big, they make the rafters groan.

I close my eyes. But he's there. Always there. Watching me.

Megan is right.

I have no idea how to stand up to him.

CHAPTER 23

'Please come with me?' Megan says for around the eleventh time.

She has to babysit her younger brother for a few hours and won't go until I agree to come with her. But what if Dad comes home early again and they pick up their fight where they left it yesterday? So I send Megan off and sit in the window nook until I finish reading *To Kill a Mockingbird*.

Paula is dragging the vacuum down the stairs as she cleans each step. *Plonk*, pause, *plonk*, pause. This is the cleanest house in the country. Every speck of dust, every grain of dirt, is sucked away until the air is crisp.

I turn the book over in my hands. I thought Ms Cusack gave me *To Kill a Mockingbird* to show me how Scout's dad stood up for the black man. But now I think that she wanted me to see how wrong Scout was about her neighbour. Maybe Ms Cusack is Boo Radley.

I go to the conservatory and take out my sketch pad. But instead of drawing, I start writing a letter to Ms Cusack.

Dear Ms Cusack,

I want to explain why I left you food. Someone told me that you didn't have money and I thought that you don't go out, so I was worried you couldn't buy food. But you do go out, don't you? And you do have enough money for food?

Thank you for To Kill a Mockingbird. The book helped me to see that we can think all sorts of things about people, but we can be very wrong.

I haven't read Of Mice and Men yet as things are very complicated at home and I couldn't concentrate. I will read it soon, though.

I would really like to meet you sometime. You paint and I like to draw. I came second in the Young Artist of the Year competition. One day, I will tell you the story behind it.

Lucy Fitzsimmons

I don't post it through her letterbox, though. I fold it and slide it into the back of my sketch pad.

Then I start to draw.

It's a woman, painting, with a cat at her legs. I spend a long time getting the arch of her neck and the flow of her skirt right. She's looking over her shoulder, like she just heard a sound but doesn't know where it came from.

172

Then I start to draw the garden around her. It won't fit on one page, so I tear out five more and tape them to the first, and I draw bushes and trees and birds and butterflies and a breeze lifting leaves high into the sky.

After that, I tape another six pages to the first six and I draw a girl, standing in a house, looking out of the window at the woman. The house is sterile. Scrubbed clean. Gleaming. It's full of sharp corners and cold marble surfaces and steel splashbacks. Only the stains of the unspoken words leave any mark, like grubby fingerprints. I write them lightly on walls and windows. *Go on, I dare you. It's your fault, Alice.* I rub them until you can hardly read them. Paula comes in as I'm doing it. She watches me smudge the word, *Talentless*.

'That woman in your drawing?' she says. 'She's a painter?'

'She's Ms Cusack.'

'Is she really?'

'Her front door was open. I went in there yesterday. Her house is beautiful.'

I expect her to give out to me for going in uninvited but she doesn't. Instead, she says, 'Yes, it is.'

I drop my pencil and turn to look up at her. 'You've been in there? You didn't tell me!' No wonder she was annoyed when I told her that Dad said Ms Cusack's house was a mess.

Paula smiles. 'You never asked.' She points her chin at my picture. 'She's good, you know?'

All this time, Paula could have told me the truth.

'Yeah,' I say. 'I saw her paintings. They're amazing.'

'No, I mean, *she*, the woman in your drawing.'

'Oh.' I look down but Paula says, 'Lucy, you are talented. Don't ever let anyone tell you otherwise.'

My drawing blurs a bit. I wipe at my eyes.

'Lucy?' She waits. But I can't look at her. I feel her hand on my shoulder. I stay still until finally, she leaves. And it takes a while for my fingers to feel strong enough to pick up the pencil again.

Every room in the sterile house is the same in my drawing. They go on and on and on. One room leads to another. But there's no front door. No way out. And every room leads back to the girl, watching the woman in the garden.

I go back to filling the spaces in the garden with thousands of tiny leaves and my head's so far away that I don't notice Mum until she's in the conservatory. She looks flushed, like she's been running or something.

'Hi, sweetie! Your father's not back, is he?'

I shake my head and she drops her bag on the floor and comes forward. 'Sorry I've been gone all day, I was … holy cow!'

She actually stops walking for a second and then comes up slowly behind me and rests her arms on my shoulders. 'Lucy, this is incredible.' She leans over me, close to the drawing. 'This must have taken you all day!'

'All afternoon,' I say. In the morning I was breaking into Hazel's house.

'What's going on in it, who are they?'

'Just a girl and an old woman.'

'And the old woman is a painter?'

'Yeah.'

'I see,' she says. She rubs my cheek with her thumb. 'Better get the dinner on. What would you like?'

'Spaghetti bolognese?'

'That,' she says, 'I can do.'

She goes back to the kitchen and I stay where I am, staring at the girl and the woman.

Until I hear Dad's voice.

Before I can even begin to think of how to hide a twelve-page drawing, his tall frame fills the doorway. 'Well?' he says. Then he sees it. 'Jesus.' He walks up, but not all the way, and he throws his eyes over it. 'That must have taken you all day.' But he doesn't say it the way Mum did. 'It's well for some.'

He leaves the room but his unspoken words stay right here. *Waste of time.*

I feel tears. I don't want them. So I force my eyes open, abandon my drawing and go to the kitchen. Mum's frying onions and reaching out for the spice rack with one hand. Dad's bent over, his head stuck in the fridge. When he stands straight, he has a beer. He twists the top off, takes a swig, and watches Mum.

'What's for dinner?'

Mum grinds pepper over the pan. 'Spaghetti bolognese.'

Dad takes another swig. 'Again? Didn't we have that on Monday?'

Mum stops grinding. She slowly lifts her head until she's facing the wall. 'No.'

'No?' he says.

'No. We had lasagne.'

'Right,' Dad says. 'So mince and pasta in a different formation?'

He's staring at her back and the words he doesn't say spread through the kitchen, *Go on. Answer. I dare you.*

She's watching the wall. The steam from the pan crawls up her face. She doesn't answer and the silence grows and the steam seeps over her shoulders and fills the space between us until it's smothering us all.

But then Dad sighs, and the steam pulls back. 'Guess I'll get changed and go eat in the Local.' He drains his beer, slaps the empty bottle on the counter and leaves the room.

Mum grinds pepper. And I know exactly what she's thinking. I can see it in the way she tongues her cheek and shakes her head. She's thinking, *He always eats in the Local on Thursdays.*

We listen to the sounds of Dad going through the rooms above us. Then his heavy feet trounce down the stairs. The front door slams, it rings through the house, then fades away.

The house exhales. He's gone for the evening.

Mum looks up at me and she raises her eyebrows and somehow, as they lift, they carry the heaviness of the room away with them. 'Well, I, for one, am looking forward to bolognese,' she says. The bounce in her voice is as surprising as if she ran after Dad with the wooden spoon. I come closer.

'And loads of garlic bread?' I say.

'And coleslaw,' she says.

'And a glass of milk,' I say.

'And a side salad,' she says.

'But not too much salad,' I say.

'No,' she says. 'We have to leave room for cake.'

'With whipped cream.'

'And we're eating it in front of the TV,' she says.

'A movie,' I say.

'First of two,' she says.

'There'll be popcorn later,' I say.

Mum smiles. 'Sounds perfect,' she says.

And it is. After dinner we put on slippers and lie across the couch with our hands on our bellies and Mum says the first movie is my choice. As we watch it, Mum laughs and strokes my hair and wraps her arm around me and it's perfect.

Then it's her choice and she says, *'Erin Brockovich.'*

'Never heard of it,' I say.

'It's about a woman, an environmental activist, who takes on these big companies in America that have harmed people and wins.'

'Now you just told me the ending.'

'Yeah, but it's not about the ending. It's how she gets there. *Who* she is. No one expects her to win but she keeps going.'

Mum hops up and rummages through our drawer of DVDs that she took with her from our old house.

'Mum? Did you like working for the bank? Back when you worked?'

She has around five DVDs in her hand when she looks up.

'God, no. I wanted to be Erin Brockovich. Or like her. Use my degree to work for a charity or something.'

'So why didn't you?'

Mum shrugs and goes back to the drawer. 'I got offered a great job, everyone said I should take it. Your dad was thrilled. Then I got pregnant and your dad was even more thrilled. We both were. There it is.' She has the DVD. She puts it in the old machine and sits back down. She doesn't press *play* though. 'Actually, I've been thinking lately of doing just that. Getting a job with a charity. What would you think of that?'

'I think it'd be great.'

'Really?' She looks like she's asking my permission.

'Mum! I don't need you to work from home any more.'

Mum grins and pulls my feet up onto her lap. 'Well, I might look into that, then.' And the way she says it makes me smile too. Because she means it. 'I wouldn't make much money, mind you.'

'We don't need more money.'

She laughs. 'What if we lost it all? Had just my income?'

But I shrug. 'I like drawing,' I say. 'Drawing's free.'

'Tell you what, you enter the Young Artist competition again this year and I'll look for a job.'

'Deal,' I say. Mum makes me shake on it. Then she leans back and presses *play*.

An hour and seventeen minutes into the movie, we hear his key in the door. Mum takes her feet down and sits forward, like she's ready to stand up.

Did it go okay in the Local? Did he find an investor?

He strolls into the sitting room and stands in front of the TV. Then he turns to us. His eyes are like fat frogspawn so I know that he has drunk a lot. 'What's on?'

'*Erin Brockovich*,' Mum says.

'Surely you've seen that?'

He watches her. She doesn't answer. She leaves the room.

He comes up to me. 'Shove over,' he says and plonks himself down. 'Mind if I switch on the rugby?' He doesn't wait, he just picks up the remote and switches.

He leans back and watches the TV.

I stare at him with the words, *We were watching that*, queuing up inside me.

Will they fight later? Or tomorrow? What'll I do when it gets from bad to worse? Tell him I have evidence that he broke the law? But I can't even say, *We were watching that*. So I know what I'd do. Nothing.

Quietly, I leave, and go to my room. I pick up *Of Mice and Men*. I start to read. When I turn the page, I realize that I've no idea what was written on the first. Because I'm not really reading. I'm waiting.

In the next second, I fling the book across the room. It crashes against the wall and three pages drop out. And the first thing I think is, he's heard me and he's going to storm up and demand to know what's wrong. And I hate myself so much for worrying what he thinks that I want to smash up the whole room.

Looking at the ripped pages, I feel so completely useless

that I want to cry. Then I notice the handwriting. They aren't pages from the book. They are Mrs Cusack's two notes, and the homeless girl's.

Standing, I go pick up the girl's note.

I hope you feel safe all day.

I trace the letters with my fingers.

'That's what I want, Dad,' I say out loud. 'But I don't feel safe all day. Because I'm waiting for you to come home. To see what mood you're in. To see what will happen. I'm always waiting.'

Taking the note back to the bed, I turn it over and over in my hands. It's going to get worse and I can do nothing but wait.

Mum's in the kitchen. Dad's sitting in front of the TV. I'm up here. And between us, the silence simmers.

I place the note on my bedside locker. Then I take my phone from my pocket and put it on top of the note.

Next time.

What use is the audio clip next time? Next time they fight. Next time he goes to hit her.

Because it will happen, and when it does, I won't be able to stand up to him.

I look up. Count the ceiling panels.

What if I didn't wait? What if I did something right now to force him to change?

I slide open the drawer in my locker. My laptop sits there. I lift it out.

Because I could do something. To force him to change.

And he'd never know that it was me. Not if I set up a fake email address. And that's easy to do.

It doesn't seem real, just how easy it is to do, but it only takes me a few minutes and I have an anonymous email address in a fake name. My heart starts beating faster as I do a search for the journalists at the *Times* and the *Independent* and the *Herald*. Anyone who writes about finance. By the time I find their names on articles, and go to each newspaper's website and look up their profiles, my heart is thumping in my ears. For a few of them, their email addresses are listed.

After less than half an hour, I have three names and addresses. I paste them into the address bar of a new email from my fake account. I attach the audio clip. Dad's bank statement.

My finger hovers over *send*. I don't click. Instead, I pick up the note again. *I hope you feel safe all day.* Turning it over and over, I think to myself, nothing will change, nothing I do matters.

But then I think of his raised fist. I have to do something. I take a deep breath.

Send.

FRIDAY

CHAPTER 24

What have I done?

It's the first thing I think when I wake. I sit bolt upright, get dressed in a heartbeat and run down the stairs. Their bedroom door is open, the bed already made.

I stop at the bottom of the stairs. Someone's down here, I can hear movement. But whether it's Mum or Dad, I don't know.

What will happen when the journalists open those emails this morning, will they ring Dad and ask for a comment? Have they already?

Maybe no one cares. It's not news. It doesn't matter. And I can't believe it, but I realize that's what I hope, that they don't care and that nothing happens. Because I suddenly have the feeling that I've just made things a whole lot worse.

There's no one in the kitchen. I go through to the conservatory.

There he is.

Head tilted to the side, sipping coffee and looking at something. Not something on the table or something outside. Something on the wall. And I get the image of a detective, studying the evidence of a case, going through it in his head, *Whoever sent that document had access to my computer.*

Dad sees me and turns slightly. He raises his coffee cup. He'll see it. On my face. In the shaking that runs from my hands to my heart. He'll know.

'You know?' he says and he squints the way he does when he's about to say something profound. 'It's not half-bad.' Then he goes back to studying the wall and I nearly crumble with relief, because I've no idea what he actually means, but I'm pretty sure that it's nothing to do with emails.

Stepping into the conservatory, I understand. My twelve-page drawing is now taped to the wall. Did he put it up?

'Gets a bit repetitive, here.' He points at the identical rooms in the girl's sterile house. 'Could use some interior décor. But it's not bad at all.'

I hear myself say, 'Thanks.'

He looks at me again. 'Really. You're getting good.' He gives me a solid nod before turning his back to the drawing and studying the garden instead. He drinks his coffee and says, 'Aaahh!'

He likes my drawing. He actually likes it. For a second, I feel butterflies of happiness. But then they sink down to the pit of my stomach, and instead I just feel angry at myself for caring what he thinks. From the kitchen, the radio sounds like mice in the cupboards, the voices are so small. But the morning is quiet enough to hear the words, '. . . *looks like it's set to be the hottest day of the year so far.*'

'Great,' Dad says. 'And I'll be stuck in an office all day.'

Behind me, through the open door of the conservatory, I see Mum come into the kitchen. She pours herself a coffee before noticing me. Sipping, she wanders over. She gives me a kiss, then flinches when she notices Dad, but she goes to the table to sit down.

Dad looks from me to Mum. 'Hottest day of the year, so they're saying.'

No one says anything.

'And here's me, stuck in the office all day.'

I don't speak. Because all I can think is, *Why did I do it?*

Mum doesn't reply either. Dad looks from her to me, and already my heart's beating faster and I'm edging away towards the kitchen before I'm forced to say the wrong thing.

I have no idea any more why I thought it was a good idea to send those files. Just because Dad was in a bad mood last night? He's better now. He's happy. And he's probably on his way out to finish a deal and pay back his loans and then everything will be fine.

Or would have been.

I kept thinking that he was going to hit her. But he didn't, did he? What if I was wrong?

I could mail the journalists again, tell them it was a joke or something.

'It's a day for the beach,' Dad tells me.

I nod.

'This is probably the last sunny spell we'll get.'

Is it? I can't think straight. Does he want me to tell him there will be more?

'When are you back to school?' he asks.

'Monday,' I say and my voice sounds as small as the mouse in the radio.

'Really?' The look of confusion on his face confuses me until I realize I'm wrong.

'Week,' I say. 'I mean, a week from Monday.'

He looks from Mum to me. From me to Mum. Then he smiles. 'Sod it,' he says. 'Let's take the day off.'

Mum raises her head like someone waking up. Slowly and carefully.

'Let's all go down to Sandymount pier and jump off the old swimming hut.'

Mum faces him properly now and Dad's grin spreads.

I don't want to. Not any more. It's what I would have wanted yesterday. Now, I just want to hide from what I've done.

'I'm mitching off,' he says. 'And so are you, young lady.' He means Mum. 'An old-school family day at the beach, that's what I need!'

Dad turns his eyes on me. I nod. He claps his hands together and rubs them, the way he does when a plan comes together. 'I love it when a plan comes together,' he says. 'Right! Grab a picnic, Alice. I'll make a few calls and we're out of here in half an hour.'

We're going to the beach.

And somewhere in the city, three journalists are having their morning coffee and sitting down to open their emails.

'You know, I don't feel like I've done this for years,' Dad calls as he gets out of the sea. The water is really shallow on the beach, but by the old swimming house, halfway down the pier, it was deep enough to jump off. And we all did, even Mum. Just like years ago. The picture-perfect family day at the beach.

Now me and Mum are lying on the sand. Mum's actively sunbathing, if there is such a thing. Her eyes are closed and she hasn't moved as much as an eyelash in half an hour. I'm lying here, actively worrying.

Dad comes up, right above us, and shakes himself like a dog.

'Declan!' Mum mumbles, but only because she's supposed to.

He grins. 'Seriously, how long since we had a beach day?'

Mum sighs at the effort of having to talk. But she doesn't go as far as to not answer. 'Too long,' she says.

'Too long is right. For the first time in months the knots in my neck are loosening.'

Are we pretending to have a happy family day at the beach or are we actually having one? I can't tell any more. Can Mum and Dad really be happy together when the words, *Go on, I dare you*, are still following them like a dog's growl? Maybe they can and I have it all wrong.

Dad sits down beside me and rolls his neck out. He leans back. 'As soon as The Old Mill is flipped, I'm taking a break. Family holiday somewhere hot, what do you say?'

'Mmmmm . . .' Mum says.

I say nothing. Just bite my lip and look away.

He sits up again, sighs, and looks around him. 'This is great, isn't it? Just sitting here?' Then he looks behind him. 'Ice-cream van, score!' He jumps up. 'Come on, let's get some ninety-nines,' he says to me. 'Alice, want one?'

All that moves are her lips. 'Yep.'

'Flake, toppings?'

'Yes and no.'

'Come on, you,' he says and then he's off and I have to drag myself up like a bag of wet cement.

As we go over the grassy sand dune bit between the beach and the pier, we pass a tent. It's obvious from the rucksack and all the shopping bags and empty beer cans, that whoever sleeps in there has been here for a while. Dad tuts. 'This sort of thing should not be tolerated,' he says.

We queue. The sea breeze is cool. But I feel like a hot, sweaty mess. I need to say something or he'll know there's something up. And tomorrow, or the next day, when a journalist calls him, he'll remember and he'll say, *You were awful quiet at the beach, was there something on your mind?* But I can't think of a single thing to say.

'Nervous about starting your new school?' he asks.

My mouth is welded closed so I nod.

Even if he doesn't get arrested, what will happen to his

business if people find out he's been misappropriating funds?

'I remember when I started your grade, all I wanted was to get on the rugby team. Nothing else mattered. You see, your old man was convinced he'd make the national rugby squad.' Dad does that thing where he lifts one eyebrow and gives me a half-grin, as if to say, *How stupid was I?* and if I was Oly, I'd probably join in. But I'm not Oly. So I keep my mouth shut.

'Yeah?' the guy in the ice-cream van says as the people in front of us leave. He's young. His face looks like it's gone too close to the sun and has burst out in hundreds of blisters. I'm not looking forward to getting spots.

'Three ninety-nines,' Dad says. 'All with flakes, and one with strawberry sauce for the little lady here.'

He hasn't called me little lady in years. It makes me think of standing in line to see Santa when I was young. That song was playing, *he's gonna find out who's naughty or nice.* A few days before, I'd stolen something from my aunty's room. I was worried that Santa knew. So I asked Dad, what if Santa thought I was naughty and didn't bring me any toys? Dad said Santa would definitely bring me toys, but I wasn't convinced. So he kneeled in front of me and said, *Tell you what. If there's a toy Santa forgets to bring, I'll get it for you. Anything you want, little lady.* I relaxed then, because I knew that Dad would.

Dad turns to me and winks. 'You still take strawberry, right?' But it sounds like he's saying, *You're still my daughter?*

I nod.

'We've no strawberry,' the guy in the ice-cream van says. 'Just lime.'

191

Dad turns back. 'Lime? Who takes lime?'

'No one,' the guy says in the same voice kids in school use to show they're too cool for whatever is going on. 'That's why it's what's left.'

'Right,' Dad says. 'And you don't have any more back there?'

'Dad, I don't need—' I say, but he shushes me with his hand.

'Where's the closest place to get it?' Dad asks.

'You could try the shop on the—' the guy starts but Dad cuts him off.

'Not me,' Dad says and points. 'You.'

The guy doesn't reply. He just sighs and looks at the next person in the queue. But then Dad takes out two fifties and slaps them on the counter and the guy's eyes focus on Dad again.

'I'm serious,' Dad says. 'My daughter wants strawberry. So where's the closest place *you* could get it?'

The boredom in the guy's eyes vanishes. 'Closest? My house. This is my da's van. He drove it out this morning. We cycled. It's ten minutes that way.' He points back towards the city. And I notice another guy behind him at the ice-cream machine. It's got to be his twin. They are identical, except for the spots. The other guy only has a few. Big angry ones, like his small ones decided there was strength in numbers and joined together.

'And that's your brother there, pulling the ice creams?' Dad says.

The guy nods. So does the brother, who moves up closer, his eyes on the money.

'Tell you what,' Dad says, using the voice where it sounds like he's inventing a really fun game. 'I'll give you fifty now, and fifty when you get back with the strawberry sauce.'

The brother doesn't say a word. He lifts one of the fifties and turns and goes straight out of the back door of the van. A second later, he's cycling off down the pier.

'And an extra twenty if you get back in less than ten minutes!' Dad shouts after him.

Behind us, a woman with a yappy Jack Russell dog grumbles about how long it'll take to get her ice cream now. Dad turns his grin from the guy behind the counter to her. 'In the meantime, I always wanted to use one of those machines.'

The woman doesn't know what he's on about and it takes the ice-cream guy a second to realize what Dad means. That Dad will stand in for the brother, pulling ice-cream cones. The guy seems to consider it for a bit. Dad slaps a twenty on the counter. The guy gives in. He tilts his head towards the door and Dad does a jump of triumph before running around the van. He hops up inside and the guy hands him an apron and a pair of plastic gloves. 'Go on,' he says to Dad.

Dad winks at me as he puts the gloves on. Then he grabs a cone, puts it under the machine and pulls. The ice cream piles out in a massive lump that barely manages to stay on the cone. He hands it out to the woman with the dog.

'I'm not taking that,' she says.

But Dad's grin comes easy now. 'I'm paying for it.'

She considers the cone for a bit. 'Put a flake in it,' she says. He does. 'I'll have two flakes. Dad pulls a face, but he hands her a second one. She takes a lick from the bottom to the top of the cone, shoves the second flake into the lump of ice cream, and then walks away.

'You're welcome,' Dad calls after her. Then, lower so she can't hear, he says, 'Cheer up, you auld bag of misery. Tomorrow might never come.'

The ice-cream guy snorts a laugh. The next customer laughs too. Dad grins from ear to ear.

But he's wrong. Tomorrow is definitely coming. And he has no idea what I've done.

SUNDAY

TWO DAYS LATER

CHAPTER 25

I wake up and I know. I just know. It has happened.

I'm out of bed and running downstairs. Passing Mum and Dad's room, I see Mum just getting up. She has that look, like her head's still asleep, but when she sees me, she frowns. 'Do I have the week wrong?' She means, am I starting school or something?

I shake my head. 'Where's Dad?'

'Around.' She straightens the duvet, then rubs her eyes. 'Kitchen, I guess.'

I run across the landing and down the stairs. Dad's in there, filling the coffee machine with water. Dad does nothing before his first coffee. He must not know yet.

The coffee machine gurgles. Dad sighs. He leans with his back to me against the marble countertop and I'm thinking, *Say something, anything, to stop this from happening.*

I notice the newspaper on the countertop. It gets delivered

early. I should have come down first. Hidden it. But Dad reaches out for it now. Unfolding it, he holds it high. Shakes it out. Coughs. Then, 'What the . . . ?'

He's turning. His eyes are stuck on the front page. He drops the paper onto the countertop, his eyes now flicking back and forward. He turns the page. The next. He stops and stares. His eyes stay where they are but his hand reaches out for his phone. He clicks it a few times. And as it comes to life, it starts buzzing and hopping with messages. He drags his eyes from the newspaper to the phone.

It rings.

He lifts his head as he puts it to his ear. And he sees me.

He's holding my eye and his face begins to disintegrate as he listens to whoever is on the other end of the line. It's like watching a dead person decay in fast forward, his mouth opens, his eyes sink and all the colour in his face drains to the floor.

He says nothing. He lowers the phone and it drops with a clunk onto the marble top, and he's just standing there, staring at me.

This is it. They know. He knows.

What have I done?

It's in the papers. It's on the radio. It's everywhere.

I'm sitting in the window nook in the sitting room. Outside, journalists chew on the rims of empty coffee cups and lean against the park fence.

Dad did something illegal. So there are consequences.

Really obvious ones. Like jail. And he's not going to just skip the country when we can't even go outside. *No one leaves this house. Not until I figure out what the hell is going on.* Why didn't I think about it properly, why did I send those files? What's wrong with me?

'Just calm down so I can think!' Dad says. But Mum is calm, it's Dad who's about to have a heart attack.

My phone vibrates.

Megan
Are you holding up okay?

Me
No. We're holing up. Not allowed outside.

I caused this. I can't believe how stupid I was. How I thought it would somehow help. I peek out of the window again and text,

I can't believe how big this is.

The audio clip was uploaded to the internet by a journalist from the *Times*. It's been played eleven thousand times and it's rising by the minute. They are all obsessed with Mr Reynolds's bank, BBR, though, not just Dad. That's why it's so big. They're saying BBR owes more than it owns, that it's as bad as Stealman Brothers. They're calling Mr Reynolds a crook. They're claiming that the dodgy deals won't just bring down BBR, but banks and businesses across the country. They're calling it a crisis.

And I did this. Me.

'How did they get it?' Dad says for the millionth time. 'Four days ago. That statement was dated four days ago. Someone must have hacked my account. They can't accept that in court.' Dad stares at Mum like he's daring her to tell him there's nothing wrong with hacking his account, so Mum keeps her eyes on the wall and doesn't say a thing.

Dad's phone rings. 'It's Seanie,' he says. He doesn't answer, and the phone keeps ringing and ringing. Dad curses. It keeps going, insisting on an answer. He waits until it stops. 'Who the hell is behind this?'

'I don't know, Declan. Someone at BBR with access to your accounts?'

'I've a guy, he works for the *Times*. Says it was an anonymous emailer.' He chews this over, then starts pointing furiously. 'I'll hire someone to trace the IP address, find out where that email was sent from.'

Oh, no. Can he do that?

'It hardly matters now,' Mum says.

'It matters to me!'

'No, Declan, what matters are all the other Seanies, all the other investors who've given you . . .'

I lift my phone again while he's stuck into arguing with Mum.

*

200

Me

He's saying he'll trace the IP address?

Megan

Oh, no! I never even thought of that!

He'd know it was me! He'd never, ever forgive me.

The doorbell rings. I jump. So does Dad.

'Don't open it!' he says. 'Those bloody journalists. Vultures. Nothing better to do than harass innocent . . .'

It's Oly. I see him through the window. He's with his wife, Linda.

Dad opens the door. They step inside in a volley of words. Behind them, journalists gather. 'Mr Fitzsimmons! What are your comments regarding the annual loans you received— '

Dad slams the door.

Oly shakes Dad's hand and they nod like two generals in a war movie.

'What the hell do they think?' Linda says. 'That you'll wander out there for a cup of tea and chat?' She goes straight past Dad, down the hall. 'Alice!' she says through the open kitchen door. She goes inside and I get up and go stand by the double doors. Mum's in the kitchen by now, hugging Linda.

'What a load of hyped-up crap!' Linda says. She goes to the kettle and fills it. She takes off her coat.

Dad and Oly come into the kitchen too. 'Thanks for coming over,' Dad says.

'Yeah, no, of course,' Oly says and slaps Dad on the back. 'Of course.'

He looks Dad straight in the eye and gives him the kind of smile the coach gives his team when they're losing.

No one notices me. Because no one knows I've anything to do with destroying Dad.

'This is the end for me,' Dad says.

'Not at all,' Oly says.

Dad and Oly go out to the back garden.

'What if it's true, Linda?' Mum says and she watches Linda, waiting to see what she knows.

'Of course it's bloody well true,' Linda says.

Mum gives Linda the slightest nod and looks away.

'Alice,' Linda says. 'You'll be all right.'

'We'll be bankrupt. He owes too much.' Mum shakes her head and looks out of the window at Dad. He's pacing back and forth, swishing a stick through the air, and Oly's talking head goes from side to side as he follows Dad.

'Look at them out there,' Linda says. 'Discussing the situation like the sky is falling in.'

'It is,' Mum says. 'The bank could take our house.'

They'd take our house too?

Oly throws his hands up in the air and Dad stops pacing for long enough to shake his head.

'They won't,' Linda says. She lifts up the newspaper. It's open on a page that shows the faces of eight developers with accounts at BBR. Dad's face is the first.

It's like I poured petrol over the country and lit a match.

'... *with an audacity bordering on the outrageous* ...' Linda reads, '... *rules which govern the many do not apply to the few* ...' She shakes her head. '*The public are outraged,*' she says. She drops the paper and looks out of the window at Dad and Oly. 'They're just outraged they got caught.'

'Idiots,' Mum says.

'Complete,' Linda says. 'And Oly may not be named but you can be sure he knew all about it. Look at them, the same as the morning before the finals in college, trying to scheme their way into passing.' Linda sighs. 'Except they've less hair and bigger waistlines now. Bloated school boys.'

They both laugh but it's not real laughter. It's more like they're sighing.

'He'll be fine,' Linda says. 'He's one of the gang, Alice. They look after their own. He'll get a slap on the wrist at best.'

Mum pours the tea and they dip biscuits. Outside, Oly watches as Dad talks on the phone. I look at Dad too.

Something's happening. Dad's face is changing. He's smiling. Not just an ordinary smile. A lopsided one. And all of a sudden, I realize something and relief floods through me.

I haven't destroyed him. He'll get away with it. Of course he will. Because in all this, there's one thing I forgot.

Dad always has the last word.

'Where on earth did they get a copy of his bank statements though?' Linda says.

'Does it matter?' Mum asks.

'I suppose not,' Linda says.

Mum and Linda go quiet again, and outside, Da

and talks and talks on the phone, his face lining with determination with each word he speaks. The coffee cups clink and the biscuits drip with tea and as the minutes pass, the silence builds up inside me until, more than anything in the world, I need to know for sure, one way or another.

'Mum? He's not going to get in trouble, is he?' I ask.

'Christ,' Mum says, taking in the reality of me. She stands. 'Lucy, honey, this must seem scary to you but don't worry, your father will be fine.'

He will be, won't he?

'Why don't we order in some food?' Mum says.

He'll be okay. He won't go to jail. I lean against the wall, take a few deep breaths.

We'll be fine. Nothing will change. We'll be fine.

Mum's eyes are full of worry as she watches me. Outside, Dad's smiling and nodding.

Nothing will change. I let it sink in. As it does, the relief begins to seep away.

It's good that nothing will change. That Dad will be okay. And it's really, really bad too. And I've no idea what to think or what to feel now.

I have to swallow a few times before I say, 'He won't skip the country or anything, right?'

Mum chokes on a mouthful of tea.

Mum smiles. 'No, honey—'

'Ha!' Dad comes in the door with his chest puffed out so far his buttons are nearly popping. He's about twenty times happier than he was left an hour ago. 'I will in my barney be skipping the country. Far too much business going on right here.' He smiles at Linda like the wisdom she's about to hear is a present just for her. 'You see, I've had time to talk it over with my good friend and financial advisor, Oly, and he's helped me to realize that I'm just another victim of BBR's irresponsible advice. And it would seem the good folk at Planning agree with me. Apparently this embarrassment has removed the obstacles delaying us and come tomorrow morning, we'll be watching the cranes rise over the mill!'

Oly's smiling. His half-time bench talk worked. His star player is back on form.

Dad flashes his teeth. They sparkle as bright as the marble countertop. 'I should find out who this snitch is and thank him. In one day's work, he's achieved what we've been trying to do for months.'

Dad takes a low bow, and when he stands again, his smile is bloated by his words.

Now Oly steps up on the podium beside Dad. 'So don't you worry, Lucy. There may be some questions raised but nothing we can't explain away.' Dad claps Oly on the back, and Oly throws an arm around Dad's shoulder. 'Your dad's not going anywhere.'

Linda actually *Whoops*. Mum shakes her head like she's saying, *You've done it again, Declan*, and Dad comes up and wraps an arm around her.

He smiles at me. Dad will put out the fire that I started and nothing will change. He starts singing, '*Your daddy's rich and your mama's good-looking. So hush, little baby, don't you cry.*' He taps his forehead with his index finger. 'One step ahead of them, baby.' Then he stands back. 'So make yourselves comfortable, ladies, because I think we're in for the night.'

'Sounds good to me,' Linda says. 'As long as there's food and alcohol involved, I'm in.'

I stay there, leaning against the wall so that I don't have to support myself.

Mum's happy. 'Red or white?' she says and she's already halfway down to the cellar. Dad's smile is as wide as his generosity. 'Tell you what, why don't I pop open that Domaine de la Romanée?'

And Oly laughs. 'Can't keep a good dog down, eh?'

'To hell with it, and to hell with them out there.' Dad points towards the journalists. 'I'm not cowering. Let's celebrate.'

And he doesn't say but I know what we're celebrating. Him.

MONDAY

CHAPTER 26

When I wake up, I stay dead still as reality settles. Outside, cars beep and trees sway and people go to work. Downstairs, Mum tidies away last night's celebration, while Dad drinks his coffee and prepares the smile he'll show to the world today. *You can't keep a good dog down.*

That's better, isn't it? Better than having him angry. Better than having the police at our door.

Dad'll be okay. He always wins. That's a good thing.

My phone beeps.

Megan
Safe to come over? I'm on my way . . .

I want to reply, *it depends what you mean by safe*. But I don't, I just say, *it's fine*.

Then I notice the time. It's 9.44. He's probably gone out. I dress quickly and go downstairs, listening as I go.

I see him. Sitting in the conservatory. He stands and walks into the kitchen talking on his phone. 'Yeah, I know … but whatever it takes, get those cranes there by tomorrow. Okay, I'm on my way. Oh, and, Oly? Tell that IT guy I want answers by late this morning on the identity of our snitch.'

My heart starts pounding. Dad will be okay. But I won't.

I imagine him coming home early from work. Throwing his briefcase aside as he marches down the hall. His words booming through doors and walls. *Lucy! Get out here!* I feel them vibrate through me now.

But buried beneath them is a voice, tiny as a leaf lying on a train track. *I hope you feel safe all day.*

That's what I wanted. To wake up and start the day without wondering, after the bottles are dropped in the recycling and the jokes are swept out by the morning's papers, what mood will he be in.

'That is why I did it, Dad,' I whisper.

'Morning, you!' he says. 'Sleep well?' He doesn't wait for an answer. He comes up, kisses my forehead and then stands back. 'Wish me luck out there, hey?'

My eyes are on the floor tiles. He's going to figure it out. He won't stop until he does. 'Good luck, Dad.'

Dad begins to go down the hall but stops. 'Bloody journalists,' he says, and turns for the back garden to avoid them.

The doorbell rings. I check first through the hall window, but it's Megan, so I open it. There are still two journalists hanging around across the street. She stands on her tippy-toes and looks over my shoulder.

'They've both gone out,' I say.

'Was it like World War Three here yesterday? God, I would have loved to have seen your dad,' she says.

But all I see is his bloated smile and puffed-up chest. 'Picture a peacock,' I say. 'He's doing better than ever because of this.'

'How?'

'Because he's Dad. He can talk his way out of anything.' I try not to look at the journalists on the street behind her. 'It's gotten too big. I didn't mean for it to get so big.'

Megan leans her shoulder against at the wall.

'He's going to figure out that it was me,' I say.

Megan doesn't answer directly, instead she winces and grabs my arm. 'You can stay in my house,' she says. Which means she agrees with me.

'For ever?' I ask.

Megan's phone beeps and a text pops up. And I see the name. Hazel.

She closes it really quickly, but not quick enough.

'Hazel?' I say.

A look brushes over Megan's face, like a trapped mouse, before she forces herself to look casual. 'Hazel started texting me last night.' Megan rolls her eyes like it's ridiculous. But she can't stamp out the smile in her voice.

'Hazel, the girl who has been bullying you?' I say.

'I know!' Megan says and shakes her head at the craziness of it.

But when I say, 'And you texted her back?' she stops. 'What does she want?' I ask.

'She wants us to call over there,' Megan says.

'And what did you say?' I ask.

Megan sticks out her bottom lip.

'Megan?' I say.

'I didn't reply, not really,' she says. Which means she did reply and she didn't say, *No*.

'You're not going,' I say. 'Are you?'

Megan shrugs and looks away. I step down onto the path and face her so she can't ignore me.

'Look, I think we should go over there,' she says.

I have to force my voice to stay flat. 'Why?'

'Because she removed all the comments. I think she probably finally realized the orchestra blog was based on her, and after what happened with Stephen ... I don't know. I think she's learned her lesson.'

I can't believe what she's saying. This wasn't about teaching Hazel a lesson. It was about Megan standing up to her.

'So now you are going to be friends with her?' I ask.

'I didn't say that, I just said we'd call over.'

'So you already agreed?'

'No! I mean, it's not like that. But, Lucy, I've been friends with her for my whole life,' she says and shrugs. 'Friends sometimes fight.'

'But this wasn't a fight. She was bullying you but now she's realized she needs you because without Lisette she'll have no friends when we start school next week.'

'Maybe she's sorry,' Megan says.

'Who cares if she's sorry?' I say. 'She was cruel. And she'll do it again.'

Megan looks down the street towards Hazel's house and thinks. 'Look, school starts next week. Hazel was nasty, we got revenge, and now it's time to move on.'

'What about next time?'

'Maybe there won't be a next time.'

'Of course there will!' I say. 'People like her don't stop.'

'You don't get to decide who I'm friends with, Lucy,' she says. Mum said that to Dad. But this is different.

'Yeah?' I say. 'Well, I do get to decide who *I'm* friends with!'

'So don't be her friend!' she says. But then she must feel bad. Or maybe she's worried that I meant it's her that I won't be friends with, because she takes a step towards me and says, 'Look, let's just go over there and hang out for an hour.'

Megan's eyes are pleading and I realize it's already too late. 'So she just wins?' I say.

'Please, Lucy?' she says. 'Please?'

I know she's going anyway. And I don't want her going in there alone. Because maybe when she sees Hazel, it'll hit her. So I follow.

When we get there, Megan rings her doorbell and Hazel answers in her pyjamas. Her hair is a bramble bush. She looks as if she's had the flu for a week. But she gives us a massive smile and takes us up to her room, and it's so weird to walk up the stairs and come into the room I've snuck into twice. I feel like a thief. A thief who stole Hazel's thoughts.

The photo beside the bed of Hazel and Lisette has been replaced. Now it's Hazel and Megan, looking at the camera, smiling.

I see Megan noticing. I see the smile that she tries to flatten.

I'm right. Hazel's won.

'Never join the city orchestra,' Hazel says. 'The people in it would just wreck your head.' She's pulling on jeans. 'I'm so glad that the concert is over.' She sits in front of the mirror in her room and takes out her hair straighteners. She pulls a face in the mirror. 'God, what a long summer. I'm so glad I don't have to go to practice any more. I mean, don't get me wrong, I love hanging out with Lisette, but I have my own friends too, you know? I just can't wait for school to start.'

Yeah, I bet you can't.

She holds a section that's just been straightened in her mouth and starts on another piece, so at least that shuts her up for a while.

But then it gets awkward because Megan doesn't seem to know what to say and I'm not about to help her.

Hazel straightens the section, drops it, and takes the piece from her mouth. 'What have you guys been up to?'

Spying on you.

'Em, just . . .' Megan gets stuck because there's literally nothing that's not a secret right now.

'I hear your dad's in big trouble with stuff online?' Hazel says with something like glee in her voice.

'Yeah, well he's one of those people who always comes out on top,' I say.

'Oh, okay, cool,' Hazel says. 'Speaking of online, I love your new blog posts, Megan.'

Really? On a scale of one to outright lie, how much would you say you love them? I look at Megan and wait for her to say something like, *So why did you write all those comments?* Obviously, she doesn't, because she's sitting there glowing with happiness.

'Don't tell anyone I said this,' Hazel says, 'but you totally nailed it. The way the people in the orchestra are so stuck up? It's perfect. What was the word you used?'

Megan searches the duvet cover for the answer. 'Affected?'

'That's it!' she says and looks at herself in the mirror. 'Perfect,' she says. I don't know if she means Megan's writing or her own hair.

She spins around in her chair. 'And you're getting so popular!' She throws her hands in the air. 'I'm best friends with the best blogger in the country!'

Megan laughs like she's just been handed an Oscar but she's trying to be modest. 'Lucy helped me with them,' she says.

'The content,' I say. 'I helped her—'

'My last blog has over four hundred views,' Megan interrupts and throws me a look. I ignore her. 'And almost two hundred and fifty likes.'

'I know,' Hazel says. 'Oh, I have an idea for the next one. Penny gets a new boyfriend! But it's not a guy in the orchestra, it's a first year, when she starts school!'

Megan's about to reply but I get in first. 'Megan already has an idea. Penny gets it into her head that—'

'I'm not using it,' Megan says.

'Really, why?' I say. 'Because of those comments on your blog?'

'Oh, Megan!' Hazel says and starts rummaging in a drawer. She takes out hairspray and poisons us all. 'Don't worry about those comments. They don't mean anything. And I think they've stopped now, right?' She waves her hand through the hairspray like she's brushing the nasty comments away from everyone's memory.

And Megan gives me a *you see?* look.

Hazel's smiling at Megan in the mirror, pretending she's not devastated about Stephen and Lisette, and desperate for friends. Megan smiles back, as if one more *like* will make her life complete.

Neither one says a single thing that's true, they just pile lies and fake smiles into the empty space between them.

I've had enough.

'You wrote the comments, Hazel,' I say. 'And Megan read your diary.'

I turn my back on them and leave the room and run down the stairs and storm out the front door.

CHAPTER 27

So that's it. Dad wins. Hazel wins.

I'm alone. I've no friends. Soon my family will know what I've done. And there's nothing I can do about any of it.

Heading home, I give Megan time to run out after me. She doesn't.

Back in the kitchen, yesterday's conversations still zing around, bouncing from polished countertop to sparkling window. *Your dad's not going anywhere. Can't keep a good dog down. Your daddy's rich and your mama's good-looking.* It's never going to change and he's always going to win.

Through the window, I see Dad in the garden walking fast, like he's on a mission.

He's back already. That can only mean one thing. He knows the IP address.

I grab my wallet from the basket in the kitchen and sprint

for the front door. It slams closed behind me but now I'm just standing here, because where am I supposed to go?

I try to catch my breath but it comes in spurts. I'm going to cry. Straight across the street is a stupid journalist with his not-so-hidden camera. I can't stay here. Turning, I run down the street and around the corner, and then I just keep walking, along the streets, through the traffic, into the university.

What'll he do to me? I've never done anything this big before, so I've no idea. But I see Mum's face, wide with fear as his clenched fist came closer and closer.

I pass the big wooden door where Mum met her friend, go under the arch and out into the crowd of happily confused tourists walking in spirals as they stare at the tops of buildings.

The homeless guy is here with his chalk out, writing the last part:

**If you can't spare some change,
spare a kind word.**

I don't see the *I hope you feel safe all day* girl. Where is she? And suddenly, more than anything else in the world, I want to know, is she safe?

'Morning,' I say to the chalk guy.

He looks up, then behind him like he's checking to see if I'm talking to someone else. 'Morning,' he says. He goes back to his message.

'The girl my age who asks for change for the train, is she here?'

He finishes the last letter of *word*. 'Haven't seen her,' he says. Then he looks at me. 'Try the station.' He points across the street.

The train runs right behind the university. I follow the line until I get to the front of the station. It's busy. I don't see her at first. But then I notice the dirty runners in a sea of shined shoes.

She's saying, 'Spare change?' to people who don't care. Then she adds, 'For the train.' In her hand are squares of folded paper.

I walk up and watch as people move around her without seeing her.

'Train to where?' I say.

She turns. She doesn't smile, but I can tell that she recognizes me. She shoves her hands, and her bits of paper, into her pockets. 'Spain,' she says.

'I don't think it goes there,' I say.

She shrugs. 'It might if I stay on it long enough,' she says.

Neither of us says anything for a while. I look around at the people passing. How much money do they give her? Is it enough? And then I know why I ended up here.

'Wait,' I say.

I feel her watch me as I go into the station. She stands outside the glass doors as I queue. It takes a while because it's busy. But she waits for me. When it is my turn, I spend all the money I won from the board games.

Back outside, I hand her the card I bought. She doesn't take it, she just looks at it like it might be a lottery ticket, but it might be a bill.

'What is it?' she asks.

'An annual pass,' I say. 'For the train.'

She steps back like I pushed her.

'Take it,' I say.

'A pass?' she says.

'Yeah,' I say.

'For a year?' she says.

'Yeah.'

'To where?' she says.

'Anywhere,' I say. 'It doesn't matter.'

'Why?' she asks.

I think about this. About the wish she gave me. *I hope you feel safe all day.*

'Because one day is not enough,' I say.

CHAPTER 28

I walk the streets. In my head, I go through the conversation with Dad a hundred times. Every time, it ends with that look of disappointment and disgust on his face. A look that'll never go away, no matter how hard I try to explain. *I'm sorry, Dad, I only did it because I thought that if you were forced to change, you might—* A woman hits into me as she steps out of a shop. She looks at me like it's my fault, like I've no right to be in her way. Then she's gone. I don't say anything. What's the point?

I just wanted to feel safe all day, Dad.

After a while, I end up at the fake nose ring stall. Megan said a bull ring would make me look tough. But I'm not tough. I don't want to see him. To speak to him. I want to run away.

The tattooed guy who owns the stall appears. 'Can I help you with anything?'

I shake my head. I can't speak any more.

'You okay?' he asks in a voice that doesn't match his tattoos. It's a voice that says he actually cares. I have to turn away because the world goes all blurry. I wipe my eyes and move on.

Dad's at home. Waiting for me. I feel sick.

But sooner or later, I'll have to go.

My hand's on the doorknob and I'm pushing into the hallway.

'It was from here.'

Mum and Dad are right in front of me.

'Declan, calm down,' Mum says.

He grabs her arm. 'The IP address is ours.'

Mum shakes herself free. 'For God's sake, calm down,' she hisses. 'It makes no sense. How on earth could I benefit from exposing you?'

She rushes into the kitchen.

'That email came from this house, Alice,' he roars. He follows her, but his words climb the walls, searching for me.

He knows. Every part of me wants to turn and run. But I don't. I force myself to go down the hall.

'Someone in *this* house created it, Alice, and I'm pretty sure it wasn't me.'

He's in front of her again.

She looks straight at him. 'Well, it wasn't me either. But whoever wrote it is *not* the one that broke the law.'

'Excuse me?' He reaches out until his finger is jabbing her shoulder. 'Don't make this worse than it already is, Alice.'

'Mum?' I say.

And she actually hears me. She holds a hand up but she doesn't look at me. Neither does he. 'Go up to your room, Lucy.'

'Mum?' I say.

She turns. There's something in her eyes, and at first, I don't understand it. But then I do. It's fear. For me.

She knows.

'Baby, I need you to go upstairs.'

'But, Mum—'

'Lucy, sweetheart, just do this for me.'

She knows. And she's going to pretend it was her. And he'll grab her and he'll . . .

She's moving into the sitting room and I understand what she's doing. She's drawing him away from me.

Dad looks back at me and there's confusion on his face. He senses something's up. Then he marches after Mum.

'What did you do?' He grabs her hard. 'What did you do?'

Mum's eyes go wide. 'I did nothing.'

He's shaking her.

'Dad!' I say.

'You did this,' he says. 'Did you think I wouldn't find out? That you'd get away with it?'

She's against the wall. He's so close to her. I run towards them. 'Stop,' I say. 'It wasn't Mum!'

The words pop like bullets and are gone. Silence swirls between us. Their eyes turn to me, filled with shock and fear and anger.

'What?' His face is as hard as stone.

I can't move. I can't look away. I'm shrivelling up. But still, the words bubble up. 'All I wanted was to feel safe,' I whisper.

His whole body clenches. His mouth quivers. 'What did you do, Lucy?'

And the other words, the ones I've been carrying for days, slip out. 'It was me. I sent that email.' They hang on the air between us. Then they rise. Swirling above us, they circle the room, too high to reach. And the silence they leave is completely empty. No more words come to fill it. There are just mine, hanging above us, waiting.

Dad's eyes bore into me. *You,* they say. But my words are sinking down now. They settle on Dad's shoulders like a soft snow, and beneath their weight, he shivers. His face flinches. His arms drop. 'What did you do?' he whispers.

'I had to.'

Mum moves. Her hand is on my shoulder. She steps between Dad and me. 'Leave this house, Declan.'

Dad drags his attention to Mum, his eyes sharpening themselves on her words. 'Excuse me?'

Then I'm aware of someone else behind me. It's Paula. I feel her hand on my back.

'I said, get out, Declan,' Mum says. 'You have raised your hand and your voice to this family for the last time. I'm leaving you, Declan.'

'No,' he states as fact, 'you are not.'

Dad is wearing his lopsided grin. He knows that he can win. That Mum won't be able to get him to leave. It doesn't matter what she says. What she thinks. He doesn't care. He won't listen.

Behind him, I see the journalist through the window. Standing around. Waiting for a story. A story about Dad. Suddenly I think of something better than a gun.

'Mum,' I say. 'There's a journalist out there, looking for a story.' I turn my eyes to the floor so I can't see Dad and I take the tiniest step backwards.

It's Mum that gets what I mean first.

'That's right, Lucy,' she says. 'There certainly is. And he's looking for the inside scoop on Declan Fitzsimmons, the husband, the father, the liar, the bully. I bet they'd love to know about all the fights, the arguments, all the times you've bullied us.'

My eyes flick to Dad's, and just like that, the lines loosen on his face again.

It's working. Dad's eyes dart from me to Mum.

'I'll back up every word she says,' Paula says.

Dad only seems to realize Paula's here now.

'By the way, I applied for a job,' Mum says. 'I got it. I start on Monday. The pay's not great. But it's enough. And it's mine.'

Mum has a job? That's what she was trying to tell me the other day! Not that she was thinking of it, but that she'd actually done it! And it's why she kept sneaking out for the last week. She really did it, after all these years. Without him even knowing.

'You can't—' Dad starts but Mum cuts him off.

'I can, Declan. And I am. I was leaving you anyway and now is as good a time as any. You've lost. And unless you want to lose your reputation too, I suggest you get out right now.'

'You can't do this,' he says again, but his voice no longer matches his words.

Mum doesn't reply. She just takes my hand and with her other, she points to the door again. Paula moves towards it first.

'You can turn and walk out there alone, Declan,' Mum says, 'or we can all go, and make a God-awful scene on the street, it's up to you.'

Dad backs away, step by step, slowly, like he's trying to find a way out of this. Mum and me follow. Now he's by the hall door. His eyes rise to the ceiling like he can't believe what is happening. But then they fall on me.

You did this, they say. And I want the ground to swallow me.

Paula opens the door for him.

'I've no problem going out there, Declan, unless you go first,' Mum says.

Dad glances out, then back at Paula, then Mum.

'I'll put everything you need out the back gate if you leave right now,' Mum says. 'Or I'll make a scene.'

Dad shakes his head. Mum nods. He looks over his shoulder again. Then back at us.

'Go. Now,' Mum says.

His face empties. Then, finally, it flattens out into the general smile he shows to the world. He turns and goes outside.

Mum slams the door shut. Locks it from the inside.

And the silence he leaves behind is as sad and sweet as the end of summer.

Mum and Paula take a few deep breaths.

'Are you okay?' Mum asks me, even though *she* looks far from it.

What am I supposed to say?

'I don't want you to be afraid,' Mum says. 'Ask me. Anything. Everything.'

I don't know where to start. I mean, is he just going to come back in the door?

'Are you okay?' she asks again.

I don't answer directly. 'Are you really leaving him?'

'Yes,' she says. She leans forward so she's closer to me. 'I am.'

But it can't be that easy, can it?

Worry lines fan out from Mum's eyes like whiskers on a cat. 'You listen to me now,' she says. 'This is nothing to do with you. This is my decision, okay?'

'But, the email—'

'I was leaving him anyway and I . . .' She looks up and tears pool in her eyes. 'I had no idea that you were so . . . that you worried . . . that you felt you had to . . .' She jams the heels of her hands against her eyes and rubs. Then she drops them and looks at me. 'I'm sorry. This is my fault. And your father's. This never has been, and never will be, your fault. Do you hear me?'

I nod because I'm supposed to. But I don't feel it, deep down.

'How do you feel?' Mum says.

'Good and bad all mixed up together.'

I didn't mean for it to, but this makes Mum cry. She hugs me tight.

I don't cry, though. I feel too many things to cry.

CHAPTER 29

Mum and Paula go to the kitchen, and I go to my room and climb into the attic and switch on the lamp. Then I go up to his face, puffed with pride from something funny he just said. 'I'm sorry,' I say. I reach out and tear it down.

I turn to the next. Anger rises off the page, the day he burned the picture I drew. 'I had to do it, Dad,' I tell him and rip that down too.

Now his face is beaming. It's the night I came second in the Young Artist competition. I thought he was proud of me. But then we went for a celebratory dinner. And I realized we were really celebrating the fact that he won the bid to develop The Old Mill. 'It was the only way things would change,' I say as I take it away.

I take down his lopsided grin. Then another. And another. I keep going. Mum, Ms Cusack, Megan; all the other faces, I take each one down until the ceiling is bare.

He's gone. He's actually gone.

And she's got a job.

This is what I wanted, isn't it? Dad gone. The chance for things to get better.

In my hand, my drawings weigh nothing. Like if I left them up here unpinned, they'd just float around in the darkness for ever. I turn my head towards the rest of the attics. Ms Cusack's and Hazel's and Mr Reynolds's. 'I'm sorry for what I did,' I say.

I imagine all the wishes that have drifted up here over the years like warm air and settled between the splinters of wood in the rafters. And I take the note from my pocket. *I hope you feel safe all day.* In the space left behind by my drawings, I pin it to the ceiling.

Then, holding my drawings tight, I drop back down into my room.

Listening as I go, I make my way downstairs. The house sounds different. At the bottom, Mum and Paula's conversation escapes through the kitchen door and wanders around the halls. It's in no hurry to go anywhere.

I pick up a sketch pad and sit in the window nook.

And I draw. A picture of a house. Not in a city but not in the country. It's in a small town. An old house, with stables renovated into a painter's lodge, overlooking a river. There's no one there. But the house isn't empty. It's filled with paintings and books and cats and dogs and birds.

Much later, Mum opens the double doors to the kitchen and Paula comes into the sitting room holding her handbag.

'I'm off, Lucy,' Paula says. She comes up to me and gives me a hug, which is the first time Paula has ever hugged me. 'See you tomorrow?'

I nod. She nods. And that's it; she goes out the front door.

Mum's eyes are puffy but she walks through the room like she's just taken off a heavy backpack. She runs her hands through her hair. 'I was thinking of getting a start on dinner. Any ideas?'

The first thing I think is, *Not spaghetti bolognese, Dad wouldn't be happy.*

'I don't know,' I say.

'Burger and chips?'

I don't care. I nod.

Mum tilts her head towards the kitchen. She means, *Join me,* so I get down and go into the kitchen.

At the countertop, I open out my sketch pad and keep drawing. The river is high and I try to make it look like it's roaring. 'Mum?' I say. 'Where is your new job?'

She pours oven chips onto a tray. 'Just up the road. It's with a charity that does a lot of online campaigns on behalf of people with no voice.' She talks for a while about what her role would be as she makes a salad and puts burgers under the grill.

'Mum,' I say. 'Are you really leaving him?'

She puts everything down and pulls up a stool. 'Yes.' She watches me. 'We've grown apart, Lucy. Changed.'

'Since we moved here?'

'Oh, I don't know. Over time, is all.'

I keep drawing. 'Do you think *he'll* change?'

I can almost hear her knock my question around her head. 'We all make mistakes and we learn from them. Your father is no different.'

I look up. Her face is open to anything I want to say. And I don't want to pretend. 'Mum, he would have hit you.'

She blinks. Looks at the wall behind me for a while. Then her eyes are back on mine. She doesn't answer directly, she says, 'I thought I could hide how bad things were getting from you. *That* was a mistake. But it's only today that I realize how much of a mistake.'

'Things would have kept getting worse, wouldn't they?'

Mum nods.

'How did you know it was me?' I ask. 'The email.'

'How did you know about Declan's loan from Reynolds?' she asks.

'I overheard Dad and Oly talking.'

Mum nods. 'Well, you let that slip so I knew you knew about the loan. And that email came from here. And I didn't send it.'

'I'm sorry, Mum,' I say.

'Honey, it's okay,' she says.

'No, I mean . . .' What do I mean? I mean for Dad. For the fights. For leaving her alone on the bottom of the ocean all those times. For never, ever thinking that she would be able to do what she did today. 'I didn't think you'd really do it, Mum. Get a job.'

Mum smiles. 'Yeah, it took a while. I didn't want anyone to know until I was sure I had it.'

All this time, Mum's been planning to do what she wanted to do. Without telling Dad. Without asking his permission.

'Mum?'

'Yes, sweetheart?'

'Can I take Art in school?'

Mum's smile turns into a frown. 'Why on earth wouldn't you?' But then she starts nodding slowly, like she understands. 'Okay, Lucy. I promise you two things,' she says, tapping the table. 'Firstly, you can take Art. You can take dancing lessons. You can take up any subject or hobby you are interested in. You can be whoever you want to be, Lucy. Okay?' She watches me.

'Okay,' I say.

'And secondly ...' She looks into my eyes for a long moment. 'I promise you that everything's going to be fine from now on.'

And I smile. Because I can tell that she's not pretending. Not this time.

'I hope you feel safe all day,' I whisper. Then I smile.

Mum stands and comes over and hugs me. And I don't want to let go. But after a while, I have to say, 'Mum?'

'Yes?'

'I think the burgers are burning.'

TUESDAY

CHAPTER 30

Mum's in my bed. I open my eyes but she says, 'It's early, go back to sleep.' I close my eyes.

Where did he sleep last night? What's to stop him just walking in the front door and going to the kitchen and putting on the coffee machine?

'Mum?' I say. I open my eyes again. 'What if Dad decides he's coming home today?'

She slides a hand between her cheek and the pillow and watches me. 'I've already arranged for someone to change the locks at nine a.m.'

'When did you do that?'

'Immediately,' she says.

It's strange, but that actually makes me feel better. Because it means she's been planning.

Last night was weird. But in a good way. After dinner, neither of us talked, like we had used up all our words for the day. We turned our phones off. I drew, Mum wasted time on her laptop or stared out the window. And the house was silent. But it wasn't a silence that waits or builds or churns and it didn't hang around outside the door when I went to bed.

'Did you go up to the museum the other day?' Mum asks.

'Oh,' I say. 'No.' I broke into Ms Cusack's house instead.

'Well, I think you should. Today.'

I know it's more about keeping me busy than getting me to draw, but still, I'm happy she reminded me, and that she wants me to.

'What'll you do?' I ask.

'Pack up your father's stuff. He's coming here at midday to collect essentials. I'll organize a truck for the rest.'

I give her a look.

'What?' she asks.

She just seems so ... confident.

'How long have you been planning this?'

But Mum doesn't answer that, instead she says, 'I'm telling you so that you can decide where you want to be when he comes.'

I think that means that she's been planning this a while.

At the museum's reception I ask about this year's competition and the lady there tells me that they'll send someone out to talk to me.

I haven't come back to see the portrait since the awards night. Entering the room where it's hanging, I sit on the

238

bench in the middle. There are two paintings and a drawing on the wall under a sign that says:

Young Artist of the Year Award Winners.
Theme: Hidden.

On the left is a painting of a box or a vase or something, all twisted up. On the right, a young couple sit on rocks by the shore, sharing a smile, with a dark storm cloud coming in off the sea. And in the middle is an old woman's face lined with loneliness. My drawing.

There's a note on the wall beside each one that talks about the artist and the inspiration.

If I had the chance again, my drawing would be so different. She wouldn't be sitting with her hands clasped and her fingers spinning time. Her fingers would be busy making time stand still, painting. And she wouldn't be *Hidden* any more. Because all the words that had built up around her would be falling away like bricks from a crumbling house.

'Lucy!' It's the woman who handed out the awards last winter. She has this huge smile and when I stand up, she starts shaking my hand like she's meeting with a real artist and not just me. She asks me about my summer and how my drawing is coming along and, with a wink, she says how she can't wait to see what I come up with this year.

'Is there a theme yet?' I ask.

She shakes her head. 'We're still deciding. It's trickier than you'd imagine.' She turns to the pictures on the wall. '*Hidden* was a wonderful theme. It can be specific or abstract. Just look at the huge variations in interpretation in these three entries.'

We both look at the entries for a while.

'Anyway, we should decide by the end of the month so that the schools can announce it in September.'

She talks for a while about the growing interest nationwide in the competition and introducing new categories. Then she leaves.

I stay where I am. It's almost eleven-thirty. He'll be there in thirty minutes. I'm not ready to see him.

'What should I do?' I ask the portrait.

My phone vibrates. I check to see if it's Mum. It's not. It's Megan, and it says,

Megan
I know you probably hate me right now, but please read this.

And there's a link to her blog. I click on it.

The Penny Behind the Pen

Summer is ending. In a week, I'll start at a new school. And looking back on the last few months, I realized something. This summer, I cared too much.

For example, I cared that I looked ordinary, so I sulked for three days until Mum let me dye my hair pink.

240

Truth no. 1. I was worried that I looked too ordinary.

Which, of course, is a disaster. Because how would I be ever be popular if I was ordinary? Then I realized something. I could be popular through my blog!

The thing about a blog is, it's not real time. You don't have to be smart on the spot. You get to think about it and play with it and only put it up when it's good enough.

Truth no. 2. A blog is not real life. You get to pretend to be someone else.

I was going to be popular. I was going to be liked, at least through my blog. But that didn't work, either. Because,

Truth no. 3. Not everyone likes my blog.

Some people do, because my blog got lots of 'likes'. But the problem was, one person didn't. She started leaving nasty comments. And she was supposed to be my best friend in the real world. Which means,

Truth no. 4. Not everyone likes me.

Now, this one was hard to accept. Really, really hard. Because I thought if I was smart enough or funny enough, everyone would like me. But now my best friend had stopped liking me. And even worse, she wouldn't admit to it! She left anonymous comments but in real life she was a bit more subtle. Things she'd say left me with that I-know-you-don't-like-me-but-I-can't-quite-say-why feeling. And in case you don't know, it's a horrible feeling.

The big truth: I was hiding behind my blog where a girl was bullying me. But in real life we pretended to be friends. So the more 'likes' my blog got, the worse it felt. It wasn't me they liked, not the real me. No one liked the real me.

Except someone did.

Because this summer I didn't realize who my real best friend was until it was too late. You see, she's a girl just like me. Except that she's not. Because she doesn't care about being popular. At least, she cares in a normal kind of way, but not in my over-the-top-I-need-a-million-likes kind of way.

Because she cares about something else. The truth.

She wouldn't accept me pretending. She made me be me. And if I wasn't, she was disappointed with me. For not standing up for myself. Disappointed with me for not being me.

And suddenly I cared more than anything I'd ever cared about.

Truth no. 5. I care about being me.

And that's my favourite truth. I can work with that. This summer, I cared too much about the wrong

> things. But this summer is over. And now I'm starting
> secondary school with one real 'like' (at least I hope
> I still am?!).
>
> And that's enough.

I'm stunned. She actually did it. The hardest thing. She stood up to Hazel, in public. She told the world the truth.

I know I'm in a museum, but ... I call her. She picks up after one ring.

'Lucy?' she says.

'It's amazing,' I whisper.

'I can't hear you.'

'Sorry, I'm in a museum.'

'Oh, okay,' she whispers too, like she's here beside me.

'You did it, Megan!' On the other end, Megan waits. 'I was looking at my competition entry and I was thinking of all the lies that were told about Ms Cusack and how I believed them and how I'm so afraid to talk to my dad and then I read your blog and, it's just so ...' I can't find the word. 'You did it. You stood up to her. Your way, Megan, not her way. Your way.'

She says nothing for ages, then, 'So we're friends?' which makes me laugh out loud.

'Yeah, we're friends.'

On the other end, she squeals.

'As long as we don't hang out with Hazel next year,' I say.

'I promise,' she says.

'My mum kicked my dad out,' I say.

'WHAT?' she roars down the phone.

'He found out it was me, by the way, but she kicked him out so I'm not in trouble. And she got a job.'

'Are you okay? Actually, wait there, I'm coming.'

I look into the eyes of the portrait of a woman who is not the real Ms Cusack. 'No, don't,' I say. 'I'm okay. But there's something I have to do.'

I'm already up and heading for the door.

Dad is at the back gate at exactly midday. We know because he texts Mum to tell her.

We're in the conservatory and I just told Mum that I want to talk to him.

'You don't have to do this, not yet, not if you don't want to,' she says.

'It's okay, Mum,' I say, even though I'm not so sure now that he's here.

'Okay, well I'll talk to him first. You wait until I wave at you to come over, okay?'

I nod and she goes out of the conservatory and down to the back gate.

Dad's staying at Oly's. Mum said that she talked to Linda earlier and insisted that Linda make Oly come with Dad to stop him from barging his way back in.

But, really, what could Oly do to stop Dad?

Her shoulders are squared. She's carrying two bags. I imagine him standing there, tapping his foot impatiently, waiting for her to open it a little so he can push her back and shove in past her.

She puts the bags down to open the gate. I still can't see him, she's in the way. But he doesn't come in.

I don't know how to do this.

Megan stood up to Hazel. I want to do the same. Tell him the truth. Not just about the email, but the other stuff too. How he makes me feel.

Just the thought of it is making me feel sick.

He probably won't let me anyway; he'll start saying how disappointed he is in me. How he can't believe how I betrayed him.

Mum's already waving at me.

I can't do this.

But then I notice my twelve-page picture, still pinned to the wall. And I look at the girl in the sterile house, staring at the woman painting.

I take it down, lay it on the table and roll it up. Then I make myself go out there, taking the picture with me.

Mum stays where she is. She smiles as I get close and holds an arm out for me. At the gap in the gate, she puts her arm around my shoulders and anchors me into place and the first thing I think when I see him is, he looks terrible.

His suit is all crumpled, like he slept in it. And he hasn't shaved. I've never seen stubble on Dad. He smiles this massive smile that looks like it takes more effort than climbing Mount Everest. Mum squeezes my shoulder and I turn to her.

'It's okay,' I say.

'No,' Mum says, 'I'll stay and—'

'Mum,' I say. 'It's okay.'

She frowns. She gives Dad a *don't you dare* look, but she lifts her arm away and takes a few steps back. I turn to Dad.

'How are you doing?' Dad says. He's trying to sound light but it just sounds fake.

'Fine,' I say.

'Good,' he says.

Behind him, in a car, Oly pretends to ignore us.

'Now, listen to me, Lucy,' Dad says, leaning an arm on the frame of the gate. 'I don't want you to worry. Everything is going to be fine. Your mother and I are just going through a few problems and things are complicated both here and with work.' He tries one of his *You know what I mean* smiles, like we are all in the same boat. 'We've *all* made a few . . . mistakes, shall we say?' He's smiling and nodding. 'But we'll sort something out.'

He's making a deal. He's saying that he'll forget all about me sending those emails and we can all get back to normal. Pretend nothing happened.

And it's really sad because he doesn't understand.

I look over my shoulder at Mum, who stops pacing and watches me. Behind her, the paint on the window frames of the top floor of Ms Cusack's peels away happily in the sunshine.

Maybe he can pretend. But I can't.

Reading Hazel's diary wasn't the right thing for Megan to do. But writing *The Penny Behind the Pen* was. And publishing the files about Dad wasn't what I should have done either.

This is.

'That drawing I drew, Dad?' I say.

When I look back, he's frowning in confusion.

'The one pinned to the wall in the conservatory that you said was good but the rooms looked a bit empty?'

He thinks for a minute, then nods.

'You were right. They were empty. But that's the thing. The girl doesn't want to live there. *I* don't want to live there. I want to live in the other house, the one filled with paintings and books, where the air is soft, where I can breathe.'

Dad nods. He's trying to understand. But his eyes search my face, like he has no idea what I'm going on about. How can I explain what I mean?

I'm using too many words.

I take a deep breath and pull out the only ones that matter. 'Dad, I want to be an artist.'

And the way his frown lines deepen, I know he's trying hard right now, but he can't figure out why that's important.

'To *me*, Dad. It's important to me. To be able to be me, without being worried or scared.' Dad's nodding furiously. 'Here,' I say, and I hold out the rolled-up drawing. 'You can have it if you want.'

'Thanks,' he says. And when he takes it, I can see in his eyes that he has so many questions he wants to ask, but he doesn't really know what they are. Even if he did, I don't think I could answer them anyway.

I step back. 'Bye, Dad.'

He holds up the drawing like he's saying, *wait*. So I do.

And for once, Dad's lost for words. His eyes scramble the air looking for some. Then he sighs. 'Look, thanks for this, and, eh, I'll definitely see you soon, yeah?'

'Yeah,' I nod. 'Bye, Dad.'

ONE
WEEK LATER

THE NEXT CHAPTER

It's seven-fifteen in the morning when Mum crawls into bed beside me. I'm starting school today. Mum's starting her new job.

'Scooch over,' she says. 'Sleep well?'

'No,' I say.

'Me neither,' she says. 'Kept looking at the clock thinking I'd set my alarm wrong. Reminds me of being back in school.' She makes a face like that would be the worst fate ever.

One week has passed since Dad moved out. He calls me, tells me that his not being here *is just temporary, until this thing with your mother gets resolved.* Mum says he has one more week to give her a forwarding address, then she's donating all his stuff to charity.

'I wonder will I make it through my first day at work without throwing up from nerves . . .' Mum says.

'You will,' I say.

'. . . on my boss,' Mum adds. She turns to me. 'Whereas you are lucky, you and Megan have each other, so you've no need to be nervous.'

'You'll make new friends,' I say.

'I will, won't I?' she says. Then she makes another face, like she's drinking sour milk. 'I wonder will there be one colleague that I just can't stand and need to avoid,' Mum says. 'There's always one.'

I don't mention Hazel. Too difficult to explain.

Dad hasn't said anything about me wanting to be an artist. But he has told me he won't be investing in any new developments until *the economic climate changes*. He still gets mentioned on the radio, but not as much as Mr Reynolds. BBR collapsed. Now almost every other bank is in trouble because of irresponsible lending. Or, to look at it another way, because of me.

'I wonder will I get through the year without being the cause of another national crisis,' I say.

Mum laughs at that. 'It's a tough one, but if you put your mind to it, honey, you may just be able to. How about concentrating your talents on drawing and making new friends?'

'I have Megan to make friends for me. I'll just draw.' Then I think about other stuff I want for this year. 'Mum? One day this week I want to call in to see Ms Cusack. She's our neighbour. And she's an artist. I want to meet her.'

'That's a very good idea. I'll come too,' she says.

'I wonder will I ever have my own home filled with my own art,' I say.

Mum smiles. 'Of course you will,' she says, 'but first, you have to fill this one.' She kisses my nose, then she says, 'I wonder will this breakfast make itself.'

She hops up and rips the duvet off me and throws it onto the floor. 'You know you are welcome to move back downstairs any time you choose?' she says.

'I like it here,' I say.

Mum throws her eyes up to the ceiling. But she doesn't realize what's really up there. She thinks I just sent Dad's bank statement, not the audio file. And I don't tell.

It's not lying. It's just some things are better left unsaid.

'Breakfast in ten,' she says.

It's after eight when the front door opens.

'Hi,' Paula calls out.

'In the kitchen,' Mum says.

Mum leans forward and gives me a squeeze. I think she needs it more than me, so I hug her back. She holds on like she's storing it up. Then she lets go.

'I'm so sorry I can't walk you to school, honey,' Mum says. Beside her on the countertop, her fruit and yoghurt are untouched.

'I don't want you to,' I say. 'I'm going with Megan.'

Mum laughs. 'Fair enough.' Her eyes move to the clock. She lifts her bag and grabs her jacket. 'I love you,' she says.

'You too,' I say.

She takes a deep breath. 'Wish me luck!' she says.

'Good luck,' Paula says, coming up the hall.

'Good luck with school, sweetheart,' Mum says. She squeezes Paula's arm on the way out and runs for the door.

Paula starts cleaning plates.

'Can we still afford you?' I ask.

'I doubt it,' she says.

I guess she's not here this morning for the money. I want to hug her too, but I think Paula has handed out her quota of hugs for this year.

She goes to the conservatory and opens the door. As she walks back, fresh air pours in. It rushes over the countertops and polished surfaces. She picks up my bag. 'You should be leaving now too, right?'

I look from her to the open conservatory door. I let the breeze flow over me. It feels great.

'Just a sec,' I say.

I run into the conservatory and open all the doors and windows. Then I go back through the kitchen and into the family room and I open all the windows there too. When I sprint past Paula, she's watching me with a question on her lips, but I keep going.

After I've done the laundry room, I race upstairs to the first floor and I open the windows that look over the backyard. Then I do the same on the next floor. And the next. Then I stop and think.

The cellar.

Taking the steps two at a time, I go all the way down to the ground floor, then on down to the cellar. I turn the latch on the only tiny window that sits at the level of the garden and push it back until I feel morning air on my face.

Then I run back to Paula and I take my coat.

'The house needs some fresh air,' I say.

'I agree,' she says.

There's a strong breeze coming through the kitchen now. I follow it past the double doors into the living room and watch as it noses its way into the gaps of the cushions, and ruffles the threads of the carpet, and sweeps across the tops of the shelves, loosening and lifting all those lost conversations and unwanted words. I wait until it's gotten into every nook and crevice and the air is as full as a dust storm.

'I'm an artist,' I whisper and my words spread through the room and jostle with all the others.

I go on through to the hall. The breeze is stronger here. It tumbles down the stairs and knocks against the door.

Paula looks at me, shakes her head in amusement, and then opens it. And as she does, the breeze roars past us, and all the words and sentences and insults and remarks that it carries zing past my cheek.

They soar into the air, up over the street, where they swirl and spin. Then a gust tunnels over the park and lifts our dust high over the city. And then it's gone. All that's up there is a puffy cloud, as white as a blank page waiting to be filled.

Across the road, a car pulls up and Megan jumps out. She grabs her bag, kisses her mum through the open window and crosses over. 'Hey, Paula!' she says, hopping up on the path. 'Hey, Lucy!'

I turn to Paula.

'Well,' Paula says. 'Ready?'

I nod. 'Yeah,' I say, and I step down beside Megan. 'I'm ready.'

ACKNOWLEDGEMENTS

If *The Girl In Between* was brought into this world with a moment's inspiration followed by a rapid write and a flurry of publishing excitement, *The Words That Fly Between Us* was coaxed towards the light with tweezers, teasing out each thread one at a time. Not as much fun, but rewarding in a different kind of way. A way that proved to me that this isn't a hobby, it's a job. And one that couldn't have been done without the support of two women.

Claire, my agent, without you I wouldn't have this job. Or, possibly, my sanity. Thank you for your advice, tireless hard work, and most of all, for being there when I need you.

Lucy, you dreamboat of an editor, thank you for waiting patiently through 347 drafts until I finally figured out what you were trying to say (and, by the end, still pretending you were excited by it all . . .). You are wonderful.

During the process of writing and editing this book, our

second daughter was born and we moved house. I owe a huge debt of gratitude to my parents for housing us and helping out along the way, and to my sister for all the babysitting. Alan and Simon, thanks for the gold and frankincense, don't worry too much about the myrrh next time.

I also want to thank all my Bray girls for staying friends with me despite *Castle on a Cloud* and all that followed for the next twenty-five years. Hickey, thanks for being so bleedin' gorgeous, and Org, thanks for reading everything.

Mitra, thank you for hosting us and for sharing your professional insights into the subtle and insidious types of control and abusive behaviour that are highlighted in this book.

I'd thank you, Chris, but, seriously, what have you done for me lately?

My thanks to the Arts Council for supporting this work financially. That support is needed and appreciated – all the more so because this is a novel in the children's space.

Finally, to write *and* be able to have a fulfilling life outside of my career, I need support, and that comes in the form of Bob, my husband. Thank you not only for believing in me, but for doing all the hard work so I can write. As for my infant and toddler daughters, you are no help whatsoever – except to remind me (on an hourly basis) of what really matters. I love you all. Now toddle off and let me write :)

HAVE YOU READ
THE GIRL IN BETWEEN?

TURN OVER FOR A SNEAK PEEK . . .

BEGGING

I'm invisible. Ma says I'm supposed to be so the Authorities don't get me. She goes out into the streets almost every day but I'm not allowed. I've got to stay inside the mill so they don't see me. When she's going she says, 'Stay away from the roof, it's a bleeding deathtrap. And don't go near them windows neither. And don't even think of leaving this building or I'll lose ye and I'll never find ye again.'

Me and Ma are begging outside the mill. I'm by the door in the shadow where no one can see me. This is as far as I'm allowed to go. Ma's out on the bottom step.

'Spare change, mister?' Ma asks a man. But I can tell from the way Ma says it that she doesn't really care. She'd rather be in the backyard sunbathing.

It's a sunny day, which means good and bad news for begging. Good news cos we're not getting wet and people are happy. Bad news cos people always give more when it's raining. They feel sorry for us cos they think we sleep out on the streets. They don't know that we don't do that any more. They don't realize that the mill is our Castle and we're safe in here.

'Any spare change?' Ma calls. There's a woman walking past her who pretends like she's heard nothing.

Ma flicks back her hair and ties it into a ponytail that reaches halfway down her back. She pulls out the front of the top she's wearing and blows on her chest to try to cool down. The pointy parts of her shoulders are all shiny from sweat and she wipes them with her hands.

Ma's real pointy. She has a pointy nose and pointy ears. Her elbows and knees are all knobbly too. She used to be much pointier, though, back when we lived on the streets.

She's real short. I'm almost as tall as her. But I'm not pointy. Ma says I've got a head like a basketball. That's why I'm so smart, she says. Cos my head's so big.

Ma says I take after me da. But I wouldn't know.

She picks up the begging cup and rattles it.

'Do we have enough, Ma?' I say.

'Nah, not if I'm getting batteries today too.' She puts it down and leans forwards and looks down the street. Then she rubs the sweat off her hands on her jeans and watches the people passing again.

Ma calls the mill a poxy hole. She says she doesn't know how we got stuck here. But I call it the Castle. It's the biggest place we've ever stayed and I think it's the best, even though it has boards covering some of the broken windows and weeds growing in between the big stones in the walls and the top three floors are so rotted that you can't run across the middle of the rooms. You have to keep close to the wall and go real slow and be ready to jump if the wood breaks, cos if you fall through, you'll break your neck.

Ma says it's a deathtrap. But that doesn't scare me cos if you fall, you just hurt yourself a bit, that's all.

'Spare change?' Ma asks a woman who's walking along smiling at nothing. She must've been daydreaming and didn't see Ma sitting on the doorstep, cos she jumps back a bit and almost trips off the kerb into the road.

'Sorry, I've got nothing,' she says, and starts walking real fast, but even I can see from back here that her purse is bulging.

'I'm bored,' Ma says. Then she says, 'Jaysus, it's hot for September.'

The sun is so high that it's right in the middle of the buildings, shining down the street. I can't even look at the offices across the road cos they're all glass, and the way the sun hits the windows is like daggers in my brain.

'Think I'll work on me tan,' I say, and I roll up my sleeves like the way Ma does and start shuffling out the doorway. But as soon as the sun hits my face, I wish I'd stayed where I was, cos I don't want to be seen and grabbed by the Authorities again. I'm never leaving the mill, not till I'm grown and have a house like Gran's to go to.

Ma sees me. 'Get back in there, you,' she says in a real low voice.

'Ah, Ma, they can't see me, I'm invisible,' I say, but I'm already creeping backwards.

Ma gives me this look, like she's sucking an egg, so I move quicker. I'm back in the shadow, hidden again. But she keeps staring at me so I look at the ground and say nothing, cos she's angry with me and I don't know why. Maybe it's cos I said I'm invisible. Maybe 'invisible' is a new Stress Word.

Some words I say, Ma tells me to shut up cos I'm stressing her out. And when Ma's stressed it means it's time to move on. I've got to go with her cos no matter what happens, I always go with Ma. Ma never leaves me behind. Except for that one time a year and eight months ago when the Authorities almost grabbed me in the alleyway. But she was real sorry after, and she promised then that we'd never sleep on the streets again and I'd never be scared again and she'd never, ever drink again. And she hasn't.

In the Castle, Ma's been good. And nothing stresses me out and I'm never scared. Not any more. The Castle is safe. The Authorites don't know I'm here. And no one else can get in.